The Unexpected Sense of Dying

LEEANNA NEUMEYER

Book and Cover design by Yours truly

Print ISBN: 978-0-9911740-6-5
eBook ISBN: 978-0-9911740-7-2

First Edition: August 2015

For my brother, Paul

CHAPTER ONE

RAINE ADDISON LAY ON THE floor of the conference room, unconscious. As his colleagues hurried to loosen his tie and unbutton his shirt, secretaries scurried to their desks to call 911. A small team of Japanese businessmen, with whom Raine was about to close the largest deal of his career, stood by looking concerned and puzzled. This was not how Raine expected the meeting to go down.

He began that morning in bed with an attractive woman; one he had met and seduced the previous evening. They slept peacefully until his alarm clock set off an insufferable beeping sound. The attractive woman stirred and opened her eyes. She pushed her hair away from her face and looked over at the clock, and then at Raine, a good-looking, thirty-three year old stranger. Feeling that twinge of shame and regret, she carefully untangled herself from the bed sheets that were in disarray over their naked bodies, and searched for her underclothes. Seeing her bra dangling from a night table, she reached and grabbed it. She then slowly moved her body out of bed and fumbled for her panties that were on the floor.

Raine lazily opened his eyes and punched off the alarm clock. He caught a quick glimpse of the naked, attractive woman tip-toeing into the bathroom before he slowly sat up and held his head as if suffering from a massive hangover. He began to stretch thinking that might help with the head pain. His body was so well toned that his muscles moved under his skin as he did this. He took great care of himself, and enjoyed having the body of someone years younger. So did the women. But stretching didn't help, and he held his head again, feeling the throb that hurt like hell and made him dizzy.

Raine had these headaches before, but chalked it up to his late night escapades that matched the long, stressful days at the financial firm where he was one of the best, if not the best, financial investors in Manhattan. A lot of influential people put their trust and money in him, and it was his job to make sure that they came out a lot richer then when they came in. He always succeeded.

The attractive woman walked out of the bathroom wearing her panties and bra. She saw Raine holding his head and asked with cool detachment, "Got a headache?"

Raine nodded. He hated that she saw him in pain. To him, it was a sign weakness. He never liked anyone seeing him weak, even if the headache was pounding now like a jackhammer. He was good at pretending nothing was wrong, even under the worst of circumstances. Once, while playing football with some friends in college, he had dislocated his shoulder after a brutal tackle. The pain was agonizing, but seeing his buddies slapping each other on their backs and lining up for the next play, he wasn't the sort who stepped to the sidelines due to some stupid dislocated shoulder. No way.

After that college game, a game that his team won, of course, when the players left the field and his was the last car in the parking lot, and after making sure no one was in sight, Raine pulled down his shirt, saw the purple and blue discoloration of his skin around the bone that jutted from his shoulder and let out a whimpering cry. He bit his bottom lip as he slowly jabbed the car key into the ignition and drove himself to a nearby clinic. No one ever knew. And that's how he liked it.

So, it was out of character for him to sit up in bed holding his head due to a headache, but the attractive woman caught him and he nodded affirmative to her question. He just fucked her, so why not be honest? He reasoned.

Without saying a word, the attractive woman went back into the bathroom and came out moments later holding a small glass of water and two aspirin. She walked over to Raine and handed them to him.

Raine looked at her, surprised by her thoughtfulness, and then said in cocky sincerity, "You're the best," as he popped the aspirin in his mouth and drank the water. He then watched as the attractive woman started to collect her clothes from the floor. She had a great body, smooth skin and long, sexy legs. Raine leaned back on his pillow, grinned and said, "You were great last night."

The attractive woman, holding her skirt and blouse in her hands, stopped, gave him a "yeah, right" kind of smile, and then asked sarcastically, "Is this where I'm supposed to say, 'you weren't so bad yourself'?"

"Come back to bed," Raine murmured with a twinkle in his tired eyes.

"I can't. I have a job. Deadlines," she replied as she started to dress.

Raine lied back, relaxed. "I have those, too, but I don't let them get in the way of – " He raised an eyebrow, seductively, without finishing the sentence.

The attractive woman looked at him, liking his playful hint. "Oh, and you have all the time in the world?" she asked.

"It's not about how much time I have," he said, "It's what I do with it." He patted the side of the bed with a smile indicating it would be worth her while.

The attractive woman felt tempted, recalling the several orgasms he gave her just hours earlier. She could still feel the faint throbs between her legs, but that was last night, in the dark. It was morning now, and she needed to play harder to get. "Only if you tell me my name," she said in frisky seriousness. Then, with a snide attitude, reminded him, "I told you it last night."

Raine looked at her a little offended, as well as stumped. "Wow. This is awkward," he said as he slowly sat up.

"What is? Sleeping with someone and not knowing their name?" asked the attractive woman.

"No, testing someone after you've just slept with them. What difference does it make if I know your name or not?"

"I know yours is Raine," said the attractive woman, sounding superior.

"You have the advantage. It's not a common name," argued Raine.

The attractive woman shook her head, disgusted that she gave herself to yet another douche bag and began stepping into her skirt.

Raine let out a sigh. "Well, thanks anyway."

"For the fuck?" said the attractive woman, now sounding bitter.

"For the aspirin," answered Raine.

The attractive woman rolled her eyes, muttered, "asshole" under her breath, and then pulled her skirt up her legs, past her thighs and secured it around her waist.

Raine watched as she did this, and then said sincerely, "I'm really not an asshole…Heather."

The attractive woman stopped and shot him a look of surprise. She found herself not only impressed but also aroused. Ignoring the fact that she'd hate herself later, she gave him a warm, surrendering smile as she loosened her skirt, let it drop to the floor, and then removed her bra and made her way back to the bed. Raine grinned.

CHAPTER TWO

THE PRIVATE CLIENT FINANCIAL GROUP, in midtown Manhattan, was in full swing later that morning. It was the epitome of corporate hustle and greed, and on the highest floor in one of the tallest buildings in the city.

Raine's office was in a corner with a full view of the skyline. He shuffled papers on his desk, antsy, but ready for action when his secretary, Jennifer, entered. She was a blonde, in her mid-twenties and professionally groomed, a cover up for who she really was, a good girl with a big heart. But big hearts never cut it in the corporate world, and she knew this, so she saved hers for after hours, and for people who genuinely cared.

"Anderson and Stein are on their way," she said with robotic authority.

"Good," Raine replied, and then asked, "Where's the portfolio?"

Jennifer spun around and left to collect it from her desk just as Raine's two colleagues, Anderson, still climbing the corporate ladder at forty, and Stein, thirty-seven and on the same ladder, entered wearing excited expressions.

"Seventeen billion dollars," Anderson said with an ambitious chuckle as he eagerly rubbed his hands together.

"And eight months in the making. Finally here," Stein chimed in with a grin.

Jennifer entered again, carrying the portfolio and handed it to Raine. "The clients are in the conference room, Mr. Addison," she informed him.

As Raine flipped open the portfolio to give it once last glance, Jennifer hesitantly added, "And your sister is on line one. I told her you were in a meeting, but she's not buying it."

Anderson and Stein gave Raine a "we have no time" look as they walked out of the office. Raine closed the portfolio.

"Tell her I'm in a meeting and will call her as soon as I'm out. Tell her I promise."

"I've been telling her that for months now," said Jennifer, tired of this routine.

"Tell her this time you mean it," Raine said as he headed for the door.

"God, I hate lying," Jennifer muttered under her breath.

Raine heard this, and with one foot out the door, he stopped and turned back, giving Jennifer a heated stare. "If you hate it so much then maybe you should work somewhere else."

Jennifer's expression quickly turned to dread as she lowered her head. She expected a verbal lashing, but Raine had that important meeting to get to and walked quickly away.

Knowing she had no choice but to follow her boss' order, Jennifer mentally kicked herself for saying out loud what she felt, went back to her desk and let out a tired sigh before punching the hold button to give Raine's sister the same, overused lie.

•••••

Raine, Anderson and Stein all shared the same power-driven and confident stride as they made their way down the hall toward the conference room. When they got to the door, Raine stopped abruptly and turned to his partners.

"OK," he began, "You two walk in first, and then I'll come in behind you."

Stein and Anderson knew Raine called the shots when it came to orchestrating meetings, as if giving plays from a football playbook, until he added, "Then you both veer off on opposite sides of the table and take your seats in the back. I'll stay in front of the room and go right into it."

"Wait a minute...in the back?" Anderson asked. I'm the one that brought them in, I should give the presentation."

"And I'm the one that brought you in. This isn't yours anymore, it's mine," Raine snapped back with a look daring him to continue the argument.

Anderson stared at Raine, surprised and betrayed. He glanced at Stein as if he might chime in and help stand up to Raine, but he didn't. Stein looked down, knowing it was a lost cause. They were lucky to have gotten this far, he silently reasoned to himself. Raine was never going to back down. Anderson shook his head at the unfairness of this and said nothing.

Raine grinned. He loved victory. "Don't worry, I'll make a recommendation for you at bonus time."

"I don't want a bonus, I want the credit," grumbled Anderson, as if his tone would get Raine to change his mind.

"Noted," said Raine. "You don't want a bonus. Anything else?"

It took everything for Anderson from calling him a son-of-a-bitch at that moment and take a swing at him, but he knew on the other side of the door were investors that took him a little over eight months to get interested in the company, let alone into the conference room. Raine was his superior. It would be his career suicide if he pushed this any further. He knew he would have to give this one up, like he had at least a half-dozen times before, so he weakly shook his head at Raine's question.

Raine stepped aside to let Anderson and Stein open the doors and enter. He hung back and began silently counting to ten before following them.

In the center of the conference room was a long table. On one side sat three Asian clients, professional businessmen wearing expensive suits and serious expressions. Two American lawyers sat across from them.

As ordered, Anderson and Stein walked on opposite sides of the table and made their way to the back where they took seats across from each other. Their expressions matched those of the Asians. A moment later, Raine entered looking confident and wearing a relaxed grin, one that implied that this was a deal he could either take or leave. He truly was the best at this game.

Raine greeted the men with a commanding, "Good Morning," as he took several steps to the front of the room, and then abruptly stopped before reaching his mark. His grin quickly faded. Something was wrong.

He stared straight ahead, frozen, with an uncomprehending look on his face. The room suddenly started to warp into a fuzzy portrait. Raine knew not to rub his eyes, that might convey vulnerability, which he would never show, but he wanted to since his eyesight was blurring and the sudden dizziness was becoming overwhelming. He turned, faced the men and tried to collect himself by glancing at one side of the room, and then the other before staggering back and pressing his body against the wall for support. A cold sweat broke out on his face, neck and hands.

The Asian clients and lawyers watched, worried and confused. Anderson and Stein thought maybe this was some new presentation strategy that Raine came up with. He was always inventing something original, and sometimes even outrageous, to throw off, and eventually win over, a potential client. When it came to meetings like this, Raine never shared what he was going to do with anyone. He liked to keep it all to himself.

A puzzling ringing sound began inside Raine's head. At first it was faint, but soon grew into a piercing screech that caused his ears to ache. Raine winced, and then tried to speak, but wasn't able to form any words. Even his lips refused to move. Panic and fear became his expression just seconds before his eyelids started to flutter until his eyes rolled up, exposing only the whites of them before they closed completely and he collapsed to the floor.

CHAPTER THREE

LESS THAN THIRTY MINUTES LATER, an ambulance rushed Raine to the nearest hospital. He lay unconscious throughout the repeated ultrasounds, CT scans and MRI's, and was still unconscious when a long, blunt needle went into the base of his head for a biopsy of his brain. He slipped into a series of comas for several days after, but never fully came out of any of them.

He laid unresponsive to all the tests until it was exactly one week after his collapse that he sluggishly opened his eyes. He was laying on his back, on a bed, in a small, private hospital room. The first thing Raine saw was his older sister, April, gently calling his name. Just two years older than Raine, she was nice-looking with a kind, open face that was now weary and holding a sad expression that she fought to hide.

When Raine was able to keep his eyes open to a sleepy gaze, she leaned forward, surprised and relieved, and whispered softly, "Hey, little brother."

Raine tried to focus on her. Her face was a vague blur. With his voice dry and scratchy, he asked faintly, "April?"

Happy tears filled April's eyes. The doctors had just the day before told her that they were unsure if he would ever come out of his coma, let alone speak again. She gasped with relief, "Yes, it's me."

Raine winced as he tried to put together where he was, slowly glancing at the ceiling, and then at the white sterile walls. He finally managed to ask her what had happened.

"You passed out," said April, keeping her answers short and easy.

"How long?" Raine asked, now giving all his strength to focus on her answers.

"About a week ago," she replied, trying to make it sound as if hardly any time had passed at all.

Raine's eye opened wider in disbelief at this, and lifted his head slightly. "A week?"

April nodded yes, as she reached for his shoulders and gently guided his head back on the pillow.

"Shit," he muttered just as a nurse entered the room. Seeing that Raine had regained consciousness she announced with urgency that she would go find the doctor and left the room.

April took Raine's hand and squeezed it. Raine looked at her. Needing to know what was going on, he asked weakly, "So, what happened? A heart attack or something?"

April managed a feeble smile and answered, "Or

something."

To that, Raine tried to lift his head again, but grimaced in pain. He carefully laid his head back on the pillow and closed his eyes. "I'm so tired," he whispered to his sister, and then let out a soft sigh.

April lovingly stroked his hair and said nothing as she tried to hold back the tears that were already trickling down her face.

•••••

It was another week and a half before Raine was fully alert. After many more tests and a bit of rehabilitation to strengthen his arms and legs, they prepared him for discharge. He looked fatigued, but was "better," as he sat with April in Doctor Katz's office, a small room in another part of the hospital. Doctor Katz was in his mid-fifties, and an expert in his field, with a compassionate yet direct and honest demeanor.

"I will be blunt," he began as he looked directly into Raine's eyes. "You have a brain tumor. It's inoperable."

April looked away, despondent, but Raine's reaction was different. He smiled, taking this as some sort of sick joke, and chuckled. This startled both Doctor Katz and April.

"You're kidding, right?" Raine asked.

Doctor Katz didn't respond. He stared at Raine waiting for his diagnosis to register.

"But I don't feel anything. I feel fine," Raine said as if that was proof enough that all was well.

Doctor Katz never took his eyes off Raine as he

gently told him, "Yes, well, there will be moments, even days, when you will feel that way, but the tumor is very real and over time, a short amount of time, you won't be feeling so fine."

Raine studied Doctor Katz. "Am I going to die?" he asked, in a tone defying that there would be any other answer than no.

Doctor Katz thought about how to answer this, and then answered softly, "I'm sorry. The tumor is growing rapidly."

Raine stared at him in disbelief. He then looked at April as if waiting for her to tell him this was all a prank. She pushed her nose into a sheet of Kleenex and tried to stifle her tears. Raine looked back at Doctor Katz, confused, although anger was beginning to rise within him.

"How long do I have?" he asked tensely.

"Four weeks, maybe six. But that's being optimistic."

April could no longer hold back her tears and began to weep uncontrollably. She choked out the words "I'm sorry" between sobs to Raine, knowing how much he hated public displays of emotion. Unlike him, she was easily broken when it came to her feelings.

Uncharacteristically for Raine, instead of a flippant, sarcastic remark about her outburst, he said gently, "April…it's OK."

His kindness surprised her, which made her weep even more.

Raine looked at Doctor Katz and asked in a tone fitting for a hard-nosed, financial executive, "So, what exactly is going to happen to me? How exactly am I going to die? Will I just not wake up one day?"

Doctor Katz looked down at his desk, the difficulty of telling Raine the truth showed on his face. He shuffled the notes that were in a file, as if stalling for time.

This hesitancy caused Raine to lose his patience and snap, "Just fucking tell me." Then he demanded more loudly, "I want to know!"

Doctor Katz appreciated his anger; it made it almost easier for him to outline the details, which he did in a professional and frank way. "There will be a gradual loss of your five senses. Your sense of smell will diminish and disappear completely; your hearing will fade until you are completely deaf. You will lose your sense of taste, anything you eat will have no flavor whatsoever, and your hands and fingers will gradually go numb, as will other parts of your body, until you'll no longer be able to feel anything."

"Then I die?" asked Raine, matter of fact.

Doctor Katz gave him a slight nod yes. "But by that time you will more than likely be in a coma."

Raine stared at Doctor Katz as if he just described a scene from a science fiction movie, and then slumped in his chair. Reality was finally sinking in.

April, seeing this, wiped her nose with the Kleenex and gathered her strength together, her time to be strong, as Doctor Katz began to tell Raine of the medications he was prescribing to keep him comfortable until the inevitable happened.

Raine let out a sarcastic laugh and said, "With all the breakthroughs in medicine, all you have is something to keep me comfortable?"

"They're for the headaches, which will be severe,"

Doctor Katz told him. "But the side effects will cause nausea and extreme drowsiness."

"So, what you're saying is for the last few weeks of my life I'll be throwing up and sleeping? No thanks," dismissed Raine in defiance.

"When the headaches become severe, you'll want the pills," assured Doctor Katz in a firm tone to match Raine's obvious denial.

This triggered Raine's anger. He quickly shot out of his chair. "What I want is to get the fuck out of here," he shouted back.

"Raine!" April called out, but Raine ignored her and stormed out of the office.

April tried to find the words to excuse her brother's behavior as she rose from her chair, but Doctor Katz assured her there was no need as he rose from his.

"You have my number," he said knowing this was going to be tougher on her then her brother. "Please don't hesitate to call me."

CHAPTER FOUR

LATER THAT DAY, APRIL GENTLY kicked opened the front door of her Connecticut home with her foot since both her hands held two large and heavy suitcases. She dropped them on the floor once she was inside, a welcomed relief. Raine was behind her carrying only a light duffel bag in one hand and his cell phone in the other into which he was talking in his obnoxiously loud business voice.

"Yeah, I'm at my sister's. They don't know yet. They're doing more tests. It's probably just stress."

April raised an eyebrow at Raine upon hearing this. She couldn't believe he was in denial about his condition, or worse, lying about it. Raine saw her expression and ignored her by turning his back.

"Until I get back, you take over...and don't fuck it up," he demanded into the phone before hanging up. He then turned and looked at April.

"Why don't you just tell whomever that was the truth?" she asked.

Not liking being told what to do, Raine snapped at his sister in an irate tone, saying he was not ready to talk to anyone about his "private life." April, shocked by his sudden anger, decided not to press the issue. She knew how Raine always needed to do things his way, even when it came to the way he was to die.

She watched with curiosity as Raine walked into the living room and glanced around, as if she were watching someone who was visiting for the first time. But this wasn't Raine's first time. He grew up in that house, and to his surprise, it was exactly how it was when they were kids. This was their parent's home. A sprawling house that had a quaint, New England, feel about it. The furniture was the same, as was the artwork on the walls and the throw rugs that decorated the hardwood floors. For Raine it was like stepping back in time.

"Wow," he exclaimed, "You kept the place exactly the same."

"Yeah. It didn't seem right to change things after mom and dad --" April abruptly stopped herself.

"Died?" asked Raine. "You can say it, you know. Die, death, dying…they're just words, April."

April looked at him, uneasy.

Raine ignored her look and continued, "Anyway, the house looks good. Left to me, I would have torn it down, or sold it. But this is…nice."

"It's home," said April almost in a whisper. Raine nodded his head in agreement. It was a relief for April to have that small flicker of momentary connection with her brother. It brought on an unexpected and overwhelming urge to weep that made her quickly go into the kitchen.

Raine watched, but didn't follow her. Instead he grabbed his duffel bag and flung it over his shoulder. He then took hold of the other suitcases and hauled them up the long staircase to his old bedroom.

The creaking of the steps made him pause for a moment. He remembered the sound and it made him smile. When he got to the top of the stairs, he took a few steps down a narrow hallway and entered his bedroom.

Raine tossed the suitcases on the bed and dropped the duffel bag to the floor. Glancing around the room, it surprised him to see that everything was precisely the way he had left it. His diplomas were still on the wall, trophies sat on his dresser, Darth Vader and Luke Skywalker action figures propped on the shelves, and framed photos of himself as a kid with his parents and sister. It was like a museum of his past, and it made Raine snicker. His sister was a sentimental sap, he thought, which he appreciated when it came to saving all his precious mementos, but not when facing death and loss.

He recalled how she was an emotional basket case when their parents died tragically nine years earlier in a car accident. They had been driving home on a snowy, winter night. There was a lot of ice on the road. Their father lost control of his car, which caused it to slam into a tree, killing them both on impact. Raine was in New York finishing an internship at a major financial company. April was home, taking a weekend break from her job in Hartford as a jewelry maker in a small boutique shop. She was the one closest to their parents, and was waiting for them to get back from a classical concert in Greenwich. She was alone when she got the call from the police and spent hours trying to find Raine, who was in a bar celebrating news about being recently promoted.

Raine didn't have much time to grieve the week after his parent's death. He was on the fast track with his career and told the attorney who handled their parent's will to give everything to April, the house, everything. He knew he would create a successful life for himself, making way more money than April ever could by making bracelets and earrings. Plus, he wasn't one to ever give much thought, or time, to the past. He had his eye on the future and that's where he preferred to stay.

But now he had no future, and wasn't used to not having one. The past was old baseball cards and fading sport pennants tacked near the ceiling in his room. As for the present, it was odd and unfamiliar. All he could do was what he had always trained his mind to do, and that was to keep moving forward, brain tumor or not.

•••••

Later that evening, after finishing an ordered pizza and beer for dinner, which Raine and April sat quietly through, and clearing the kitchen table in the same, silent way, they sat across from each other once again to go over their "future."

Carefully spread out in front of Raine was his papers and documents. He dutifully explained each one to April as she watched, trying hard to match his calculated professionalism, although inside it was killing her.

"Here is the title to my apartment in Manhattan. It's all paid for. I got people always approaching me to buy it, so if you do sell it, make sure you get top dollar. Don't let anyone hustle you. Get yourself a good agent. And here are my bank books. I have four accounts. This is the list of the banks and the account numbers. My life insurance policy is here," he said tapping his fingers on a thick document.

He then pushed aside a black address book as he reached for a business card and held it out to April. "I already contacted my attorney. Here's his card. He knows what's going on. I told him. And he knows everything is being left to you."

The strain of composure became too much for April, so she hung her head down and began to cry. Again, she knew this was exactly what Raine hated, so she murmured softly, "I'm sorry…I'm sorry," as she wiped her tears away.

Raine looked at her sympathetically, but wouldn't allow himself to give in to feeling sorry for her, or himself. "April…don't," he said with mild authority.

But April could hold it in no longer and shouted, "No!" as she pushed her seat away from the table in anger and cried, "This is wrong! You're my baby brother. It should be me."

This triggered Raine's anger. Losing his composure, he shouted back, "Stop it! Just stop it!" slamming his hand on the table.

April quickly stood, turned and grabbed a sheet of paper towel from a nearby roll, wiped her eyes, and then held it to her mouth. Raine, unable to deal with any of this, got up and stormed out of the room.

With him gone, April was finally able to let go and began to sob uncontrollably. She turned, leaned over the counter and shook her head, whimpering, "Why, God? Why?"

Suddenly, the song "Badlands" by Bruce Springsteen came blaring from the living room. This caused April to stop crying and look up in confusion. She made her way out of the room and followed the music. When she reached the living room, she saw Raine standing in a corner, flipping through a stack of CD's as the song blasted from the stereo speakers.

April shouted at him to turn it down. Raine didn't hear her. She shouted a second time, louder. He still didn't hear over the loud drums and piercing guitars. Frustrated, she made her way over to the stereo and abruptly turned it off.

Raine spun around and shouted, "Hey!"

"I have neighbors!" April snapped.

"Me, too. In Manhattan they didn't give a shit," Raine said without concern.

"Well, this is Connecticut. We give a shit!" said April, now fuming.

Raine liked seeing April for once not being an emotional wreck, and smiled at her remark. He then held up the Springsteen CD. "He's the best, isn't he?"

"God, you say that about everything," answered April, unimpressed.

"What do you mean?" he asked.

"You always say 'the best'. As kids we'd go out to eat, and after you'd say, 'that was the best restaurant."

"It probably was," said Raine with a shrug.

"Every restaurant?" April asked, making her point.

Raine looked at her, wondering why she was

bringing it up.

"It's just something you always say," she said sadly, "I guess I'm just realizing it now."

She hoped he wouldn't see that she was trying to save every detail, past and present, of her dying brother. Seeing him looking at her, she made a playful attempt to keep the conversation light.

"What isn't the best with you?" she asked him.

"A brain tumor," he said dryly.

The fragile, playful moment took a fast nosedive. Tears filled April's eyes. Without saying a word, she walked out of the room.

CHAPTER FIVE

THAT NIGHT, RAINE SAT ALONE in his bedroom. The silence was deafening, unlike the brazen city sounds of Manhattan that so easily distracted him. He wasn't used to this, nor used to being able to hear his own thoughts. Thoughts that he didn't want to hear, and did all he could to avoid.

He saw a baseball mitt with a ball in it lying on a corner shelf. He quickly got off his bed, grabbed the mitt, sat back down and began tossing the ball in the air and catching it with the mitt. It felt good to recall his youth and baseball. He hadn't played since he left Connecticut. He didn't even try out for it in college, or play it for sport on weekends. Football became his game of choice mostly due to the new crowd he surrounded himself with, the financial wolves. Baseball wasn't for those types, so he left it behind...much like everything else from his past.

He tossed the ball high in the air and caught it in the mitt, but didn't feet any sensation when it hit his hand. He pulled his hand out of the mitt and shook it, looking worried. He rubbed his hand against the mitt, trying to regain feeling. Nothing. He wiggled his fingers and made a fist several times, but to no avail. His hand was numb and this scared the shit out of him. Was the tumor really growing that fast? He wondered.

Defying his condition, he put one side of his hand in his mouth and bit down. Still nothing. As fear gradually turned into panic, Raine threw the mitt on the bed, got up and went over to his desk. He held out his hand and, with all his strength, slammed it down hard. He shut his eyes and winced in great agony, trying not to scream. Obviously, the feeling came back. He held his now throbbing hand close to his chest as he sat back on the bed and tucked it between his legs, rocking back and forth, still in pain.

Once it subsided, Raine held out his hand and looked at it. Just seconds ago it was completely numb, now he had feeling back. Was this how it will be from here on out? He questioned. And in that instant, reality hit him hard. He was going to die. He had been able to dismiss this truth for a good amount of time, but now it was suddenly very, very real. Staring at his hand, he fought back tears, but it was useless. He curled himself up in a fetal position, grabbed his pillow and started to sob uncontrollably into it.

CHAPTER SIX

RAINE MADE NO MENTION TO April about losing feeling in his hand. He didn't want to see any waterworks from her, but it still bothered him, as he sat slouched on the back porch the next day, staring out at the large, well landscaped property of his youth wondering which part of himself he would lose first. He then stared up at the clear, blue sky, taking in the splendor of it. It was one of those days that defied anything unpleasant to occur, or even exist, such as death, he thought. Life was such a very strange thing.

Just then, April came out carrying a tray of sandwiches and a pitcher of iced tea. "I made tuna sandwiches just the way you like it, with chopped apples...and some iced tea with orange juice," she said as she set the tray down on a folding table next to Raine.

Raine looked at her, impressed and delighted. He couldn't remember the last time anyone made anything for him, let alone to his perfection. He sat up, excited,

"Thanks. This is the – "

"Best?" April interjected with a chuckle.

Raine looked at her and smiled. Maybe he did say that a little too much. Just then, the doorbell rang.

"Oh, that's Guy. I'll be right back," April announced happily as she dashed back inside the house.

As Raine reached for one of the sandwiches his expression turned to confusion. "Guy?" he muttered to himself as he looked toward the house. He then shrugged, returned to his sandwich and took a bite. The crunch of the apple with the salty taste of tuna was heaven in his mouth. He rolled his eyes in delight, having forgotten the little things that he used to so enjoy.

As he savored the sandwich, April stepped out on the porch, smiling. She was with Guy, a good looking, athletically built man in his mid thirties.

"Raine…this is Guy," April said proudly. "Guy, this is my brother, Raine."

Guy gentlemanly stepped forward and held out his hand to shake Raine's. Raine wiped his hand on his pant leg and shook Guy's hand hard.

"It's nice to finally meet you," said Guy sincerely.

Raine, unimpressed, joked in a cocky manner, "I never met a 'Guy' before. What happened? Your parents couldn't come up with a real name?"

April was too embarrassed to speak, but Guy took it all in playful stride by replying, "And the best your parents could come up with was Raine?"

"We were both born in April," Raine explained. "Get it? April, Raine?"

"My mother thought it was cute," April added, still

embarrassed.

Guy looked at April, lovingly. "It is," he said with a smile.

"So, what do you do – Guy?" asked Raine, still sounding cocky.

"I'm a fireman," Guy proudly responded.

"Wow. A fireman," said Raine. He looked at April, and then purposely to embarrass her added, "Hot."

April rolled her eyes, now mortified. Raine enjoyed getting his older sister to blush, his way of being playful with her.

"So how long have you two been...?"

"Almost a year," answered Guy.

"We're engaged," said April.

Raine was quickly taken aback. Her announcement was completely unexpected. He looked at April, insulted. It was one thing that she had a boyfriend, but she had never mentioned she had a fiancé.

April noticed Raine's shocked expression, looked at Guy and said softly, "Guy, can you …"

Guy didn't let her finish the sentence. He knew she needed to talk to her brother, so he quietly went back inside the house. Once he was gone and out of hearing range, Raine tossed his sandwich over the porch railing and said angrily, "What the fuck, April? I meet this guy for the first time and you're engaged to him?"

"I tried to tell you," she said, frustrated. "That's why I've been calling for the last several months, but you were too busy to talk to me."

"I was working!"

"All the time?"

"You didn't try hard enough," Raine said, fuming.

"Are you kidding me? I left dozens of messages at your apartment, at your job, and now it's my fault you were too busy?"

"I'm not busy anymore," he replied in a cutting tone. "Now I'm just dying."

His words threw April. She looked at him with hate and sympathy. Tears filled her eyes, but before they fell she quickly went back inside the house. Raine turned and stared out at the lawn, loathing himself for what he had said, but more for never having returned her phone calls.

Inside, April went looking for Guy. She found him in the kitchen making a sandwich. She entered looking visibly shaken and wiping away tears.

"You all right?" he asked, quickly putting down the sandwich.

"It's all so sudden," April said, exasperated. "I love him. I want to take care of him. But then...I'm going to lose him. It's happening too fast."

As she started to cry, Guy took her in his arms and held her close.

CHAPTER SEVEN

RAINE SPENT THE REST OF that day and night in his room. He couldn't be around April, and had no interest in getting to know Guy. He hated how his life was suddenly turned upside down and felt like a prisoner in his old bedroom, but more so in his deteriorating body. He ignored April the few times she came to the door and knocked asking if he wanted dinner, or watch a movie. He barked, "Leave me alone," when she persisted, and then felt like an asshole when he heard her footsteps and sniffles move away. He didn't mean to take it out on her, but he was dying for Christ's sake! Didn't she understand that? Until he had a better handle on it, he wanted to be alone. But how and when does anyone ever get a handle on dying? He wondered.

Raine slept late the next morning. He didn't feel like getting out of bed, so he dozed for a few hours before finally forcing himself up and taking a shower. His laziness was partly due to the tumor since it made him fatigued, but mostly because he felt like shit. He knew he hadn't been the ideal brother, and hated how much time he'd let come between himself and his sister.

It was close to noon before he finally dressed and went down the stairs to get something to eat. He stopped halfway on the staircase when he saw Guy and April setting up festive decorations near the front of the house and living room.

"What's going on?" he asked, puzzled.

"We have our engagement party tonight," April said as she stood on a stepladder, tacking up streamers. She glanced over her shoulder before turning back, not interested in his reaction. She was sore by his behavior, yet it bothered her that there was no immediate, typical comeback from him, so she looked over her shoulder again and said in a snide tone, "I sent you an invitation. Four to be exact."

Raine shook his head in regret. Obviously he never opened any of them. April suddenly felt bad. Being bitchy wasn't her nature, and she hated herself for it. She looked over at Guy for help in what to do. He just shrugged.

Feeling guilty, as well as a slew of other mixed emotions; April let go of one of the streamers and gave in. She turned to Raine and said, "I'm sorry. I can cancel the party..."

"No, no. Don't do that. It's your party," he said, being supportive and generous, although the last thing he wanted to deal with was a house full of strangers.

"But you're..." she started to say, but couldn't let out the word "sick," so she quickly turned her attention to Guy. "I think we should cancel."

"No!" shouted Raine with authority. "I'll just stay in my room."

"But you've been in there since yesterday! We want you to come, Raine. It'll be small anyway," said April, trying to downplay what she had planned for months as a huge event for her and Guy. "Just a few friends."

Then she suddenly had an idea as she began to step down from the ladder. "Hey, why don't you call some of your friends?" she asked, hoping he'd agree.

"No," said Raine, flatly.

April didn't want to let the opportunity to meet some of Raine's friends go. "No, really, call your friends. I think they'd love to see you. We're not far from New York."

"No," said Raine again, growing edgy.

Not wanting to push the point, but curious just the same, April said gingerly, "You haven't called one person. I'm sure your friends are wondering what's going on. Don't you think —"

"I said no!" shouted Raine. "I don't want pity. I don't want anyone seeing me...or watching me...or acting like I'm not going die!"

Guy awkwardly looked down at the decorations in his hands. April felt wounded and distraught. Raine saw this, which bothered and disgusted him.

"I'm going to go lie down," he said as he turned to go back up the stairs.

"Raine — " started April, hoping to ease the conflict, but Raine stopped her.

"Just leave me alone, April. Have your damn party, but just leave me alone," he snapped. And with that, he turned and walked back up the stairs.

The sound of his bedroom door slamming shut was heard a moment later. April slowly went back to hanging the decorations as she fought back tears. Seeing this, Guy quietly put down his decorations and headed slowly up the stairs. When he reached Raine's door, he knocked.

Raine shouted at the door, "What?"

When Guy opened the door he saw Raine standing by the window. Raine turned; surprised to see it wasn't April. Guy walked toward him with a determined attitude.

"April didn't want to have the party when she found out about your condition, but I told her she needed it. I'm making her do this, so blame me."

"I'm not blaming anyone," said Raine grumpy, leery of Guy's intention.

"Then stop acting like a fucking asshole and treat your sister with some respect," he said, sounding threatening.

Taken aback, Raine noticed that Guy was inches taller than he was, and with muscles much more solid.

"She's doing her best to make you comfortable. And if you can't appreciate it, even a little, then you can go back to New York and die there." Guy took a beat, and added, "I don't know you, and it doesn't look like there's much time to even get to know you, but you mean a lot to April, though I've seen no evidence of why, and she means a lot to me, so hide up here if you want, but April needs her friends now so she can have the support and strength to take care of you."

With that, Guy turned and left the room. There was no allowing Raine to respond. Guy didn't care what he had to say. Raine stood there stunned and contemplative.

Downstairs, Guy entered the dining room where April was clearing away the things on the table that belonged to Raine, all the papers and documents he was showing her from the previous evening. She stopped when she saw Guy and asked if Raine was all right.

"I don't know," he answered. "I think so. Are you?"

"I just hate that he's cutting himself off from everyone. I mean, I suppose I get it, but I wish he'd call at least one friend to come. I'm sure they're wondering what's going on."

After saying this, she realized she had Raine's black address book in her hand and looked at it. "Fuck it. Life is short as it is. I'm inviting someone he knows. He can't shut people out. By the time he does want them, or needs them, it'll be too late."

She put the black address book on the table and opened it. Guy went around and stepped up next to her. "Do you really want to do that?"

"If he gets mad at me, I don't care anymore," she said as she started to search inside the book. "He's mad at me anyway." Her finger moved down a page, and then another as she murmured, "City Florist...Drake's Plumbing...Consuelo Garcia? Oh, that's his housekeeper."

Guy stood next to her, peering over her shoulder at the names as well.

"Ray Harris, that's his attorney. Jeez, I'm not sure whom to invite. It's all businesses and dry cleaners," April said, perplexed.

Guy took the address book from the table and flipped through the pages.

"I can't find one name," said April.

"Because there aren't any," said Guy, looking up from the book. "April...Raine has no friends," he whispered, sad and low.

April looked at Guy in disbelief. How could that be? He was a huge financial wizard in Manhattan. He boasted constantly about whom he knew and mingled with every chance he got. It didn't make any sense.

"He has no friends," Guy repeated before the words began to sink in for April.

CHAPTER EIGHT

THAT NIGHT, APRIL FOUND HER home filled with a warm community of friends, as well as a lot of Guy's family members and fellow firefighters. They were all gathered in the living room, drinking and sharing stories. Guy sat in a large, cozy chair with April perched on the arm of it, close to him. A colleague and buddy of Guy's, a robust, witty loud mouth, egged Guy on to tell everyone how he and April met.

"Oh, you've all heard the story," said Guy shaking his head, tired of repeating it.

"Not the real story," said his buddy letting out a knowing laugh, which caused the group to shout out pleas for Guy to share it.

Guy groaned. April laughed and nudged him to stand and tell it. Shaking his head, Guy lazily stood looking embarrassed. As he did this, Raine, tired of being in his room and curious about the party, quietly made his way down the stairs, peered inconspicuously in the room and listened.

Guy cleared his throat and began, "OK…the real story. There was a fire across the street from where April worked. After we put out the blaze, I was going back to the truck and there was this crowd of people outside watching. I saw April in the crowd and thought she was the prettiest girl I'd ever seen." Guy looked over at April and winked. "I just had to meet you."

The guests all laughed and gave out appreciative "Aww's".

"So, I had to think fast," Guy continued. "I grabbed a clipboard from the truck. It had one piece of paper on it, the list of our lunch orders that day. I flipped it over and walked across the street acting all official, as if I was the chief or something. I told everyone I had to get their names and numbers as possible witnesses."

He let out a laugh, as did everyone else in the room, and then cleared his throat again and said, "I must have taken down about ten names before I got to April. Hers was the only one I wanted."

April covered her mouth, trying to hide her laugh. Raine saw this from where he was standing and smiled. He had not seen his sister smile in a long time, especially in the last few days.

"So, I took her name down and said, 'Can I call you tonight?" said Guy finishing his story.

April quickly interjected. "No, you said…" she imitated his deep voice, "I'll be at the station late tonight, gathering evidenced. If you're available to come down to fill out a full report that would be really helpful."

Several of the guests shouted out, "Real smooth,

Romeo" and "What a line!" as they busted out laughing. Guy lowered his head, guilty.

A female friend asked April, "Did you go?"

April blushed and said sweetly, "Yes."

The room broke out in laughter and applause. Raine silently chuckled, shaking his head. His sister always fell for corny lines.

"But I knew he was hitting on me," said April in her defense.

"How?" Guy asked, surprised.

"Who collects evidence for a grease fire in a diner that took less than two minutes to put out?" answered April with a grin. "Some 'blaze'!"

Again the room erupted in laughter.

"But you showed up!" said Guy, trying to make her look sillier than he did.

"And the fire's been burning ever since," she said rolling her eyes, knowing it was a cliché thing to say.

Everyone laughed and applauded again. Yes, it was a cliché, but sweet. Another friend then raised a glass.

"To Guy and April!"

Everyone in the room all raised their glasses, toasted, and cheered. Raine was visibly moved, but also felt oddly out of place, so he quietly disappeared away from the entrance and made his way back up the stairs. April saw Raine from across the room, and felt a sudden stab of sadness seeing him leave, but maintained her happy demeanor for her guests and Guy.

•••••

Hours later, after the last guest had left, Guy had his arm around April's waist, as they stood at the front door.

"I'm the luckiest guy in the world," he said before he kissed her. It was a long, satisfying kiss.

When April pulled away, she asked, "Are you sure you can't stay?"

"I wish. I have early duty. I'll see you tomorrow night?"

"You better," April answered as she gave him a playful punch to his chest.

They kissed once more, and then Guy stepped outside and made his way to his truck. April watched him, lovingly. She waved, and then closed the door. Letting out a heavy sigh, she walked into the kitchen. She began to collect the dirty plates and cups, placing them into the sink and started to run the water. As she did this she looked out the window that had a perfect view of the backyard and saw Raine standing at the end of the porch, staring up at the night sky.

April turned off the water, wiped her hands on a dishtowel and went to the back screen door. She opened it, stepped out on the porch and slowly approached Raine.

Sensing someone behind him, Raine turned, saw his sister and said a soft, "Hello."

April said hello back, but in a sharper, unfriendly tone. Raine didn't notice.

"That was a nice party. I caught a little of it," he said.

"Yeah. I saw you," April said disinterested.

"You have a lot of friends. Good friends," Raine said with a hint of relief in his voice.

"Yes. I do," said April, now with irritation in her voice.

"I'm glad. It's important."

"Is it?" snapped April, her anger building.

Raine, finally detecting something was wrong, answered with a simple, "yeah."

April, not wanting to give into her anger, walked to the other edge of the porch and leaned against its railing. She lowered her head, frustrated.

"Are you OK?" asked Raine.

"No," she said, looking up.

"What's wrong?"

April tried to control her temper as she gave her answer. "What's wrong? You! That's what's wrong. Why didn't you want any of your friends to come here tonight?"

Raine looked away, tired. "I told you. I don't want people feeling sorry for me."

"No, that's not true, Raine. It's because you don't have any friends," April shot back, her anger beginning to show.

"I have friends," said Raine defensively.

"No you don't! I looked in your address book to invite someone here to cheer you up, but there wasn't one person in it that doesn't serve you," snapped April.

"You're going through my stuff now?" asked Raine wanting to have something to fight back with.

But April was too fed up to care and shot back, "Oh, sorry…should I have waited until you were dead?"

This jolted Raine. He'd never seen April this angry before.

"I didn't want to wait until then, Raine, because

then it's too late. I didn't want to pick up the phone in a few months and have to tell total strangers that you're gone."

Raine looked away, bothered and caught, hoping she would shut up, but April wasn't about to back down.

"Why don't you have any friends?" she asked angrily.

"I was busy," Raine snapped back. "In my line of work you don't have time to make friends."

"No time to make friends?" repeated April. She looked at him, disgusted and asked in a pathetic tone, "Who are you?"

Sounding like a swarthy salesman, Raine answered, "There are no friends in finance, April. It took every waking moment for me to make the kind of money I made. The competition out there is fierce. You so much as blink and someone is right behind you ready to take you down."

"And you never once stopped to think that one day it would end?" April asked, knowing the answer.

"No, I didn't. I'm thirty-three! Forgive me if getting a brain tumor was not something I gave much thought to."

April looked down at her feet, shaking her head. Raine stared out at the backyard, pissed off. Slowly, his mood softened and he asked, "What does it matter now anyway?"

His words infuriated April. She looked up, enraged. "It matters a lot, you fucking jerk! You're leaving me with nothing!"

"What do you mean, nothing? You're getting everything! My life insurance, all my money...that apartment in New York alone is worth —"

"I don't care about your God damned apartment!" shouted April. "Whom am I supposed to call a week after you're dead? When I'm sitting here alone, missing you and need to reach out to someone who knew you, so I can feel close to you again so you're not some distant, fading memory. Who do I call six months from now so I can say, 'hey, remember when Raine used to'...or a year from now...or five years from now? That's how you keep people you love alive after they're gone...something to hold on to so death doesn't feel so fucking final!" She took a step toward him. "But you've made it final for me, Raine. You left me with nothing. So, fuck your money...fuck your apartment in New York...and fuck *you*, you selfish prick!"

Tears formed in her eyes, but not from sadness. Instead it was anger and she wasn't about to stand there and have him think she was sad. Not this time. No, she was angry. But even more than that, she was hurt. Her body shaking from raw nerves, and nothing else to say, she stormed back inside the house, slamming the screen door behind her.

Raine stood on the porch frozen from her words. Never had April spoken to him like that before. He felt the instinct to go inside and calm her down, maybe even discuss it, but what was there to discuss? She was right. Raine had no friends. He was alone, and he'd known it for years. It never bothered him until that moment because now he knew he had dragged his sister involuntarily into his empty misery.

CHAPTER NINE

RAINE LIED AWAKE IN BED that night, unable to sleep. Restless, he got up, grabbed the baseball mitt again and started to toss the ball in the air as he paced the room. Everything April said to him earlier weighed heavily on his mind. The two of them were so close when they were kids, and although he was two years younger than she, he always played it as if he were the protective older brother. He was more confident and in control then she was, especially with his emotions. He hated it when she cried, and used to do anything to prevent it. If it meant buying her an ice cream when she was upset, or punching out a boyfriend that got out of line, he did it.

That's also how he showed that he loved her. He didn't know any other way how. They began to drift apart when he went away to college, and then on to that internship in Manhattan. It had nothing to do with any sort of falling out. They just went in separate directions. He was more focused on making something of himself. Their father was a lawyer and taught him about hard work, finances and, most importantly, how to shut out emotion when it came to business. There was no room for sentiment when making a deal. It was never personal. Just get the job done. That was the rule.

The last time either of them spent a good amount of time together was when their parents died. April had phoned Raine immediately, but wasn't able to reach him until the early morning hours. He was in a loud bar celebrating a promotion with friends and blissfully ignored the texts and phone messages that were being left on his cellphone until he finally heard his phone ring and picked up. He felt some guilt when he heard the news, but managed not to give in to it. He had a funeral to plan with his sister. Just get the job done.

April was too shattered over the loss to care about Raine not responding to her desperate calls, and never commented about it even after their parent's funeral. She was too consumed with despair and was happy to have Raine take charge, so she felt she owed him never to ask. And taking charge was something that came easy to him since he handled it as just another business transaction, and was again able to keep his emotions out of it, though he did struggle with the occasional thought of the unfairness life had just been handed to himself and his sister, let alone his parents.

Raine and April's father was close to retiring from his law firm before his death, and had made plans for he and his wife to start looking for a vacation home someplace near the ocean. He had spent almost all of his time working and little time at home. He had felt some guilt about that, but was successful at telling himself that his focus was "needed" on making a comfortable home for his wife and two kids. Attention, love and care were his wife's job, and that's how it was split.

There were the two-week vacations every year, and long holiday weekends to enjoy with his children. To him that was enough. As far as communication, he was at his best when discussing law ethics and financial investments. Anything else, such as the domestic chores of the house, or his children's schooling, he would quietly listen and nod or shake his head when he agreed or disagreed.

As Raine paced the room and tossed that baseball, he thought about his father and how much he had become just like him. He had a hysterical, angry sister downstairs and he didn't know how to handle her. Especially when she was right. He didn't want to be a burden to anyone, and now somehow he had become the biggest one of all. It was unfair to April, and all the money and material things he had planned to leave behind to guarantee her a comfortable life suddenly wasn't enough.

But he had nothing else to give. The only thing he had of any value, he thought, was time. And there wasn't much left of that either. For the first time he felt truly fucked and was unable to come up with some idea or plan to pull himself out. He put down the ball and mitt, and lied on his bed. He wondered was this all that was left of his life? Lying on this bed, engulfed by these four walls until he became a drooling vegetable doped up on meds until his organs finally shut down for good? Was that all he was going to leave his sister? The thought was agonizing. It made his chest feel like it was in a vice being squeezed tight, as his guts turned into a thousand knots. He had never felt so disgusted with himself.

For a moment, and it was only a fleeting moment, he thought about ending his life. A series of quick ideas flashed through his mind like postcards: Jumping off a building, blowing his brains out with a gun, overdosing on his meds, slashing his wrists, driving in front of a train. Then he stopped. That was bullshit, he thought. He hated himself for even letting his imagination run away like that. That wasn't the way out of this. In fact, he knew there was no way out, but he had to make it bearable, but not just for himself…for April.

He began to think hard about what he would say to her in the morning. He knew he had to say something meaningful. Heartfelt. The truth. He had never expressed himself in such a way before and the idea frightened him.

Getting an idea, he got up, went over to his desk, opened a side drawer and pulled out a sheet of paper and a pen. He stared at the pen in his hand, and slowly rolled it between his fingers. He appreciated its grooves as he gripped it, clicking it open and clicking it closed several times. It was such a small object, he thought, one he has handled thousands of times in his life, but this one had him captivated because, "One day," he whispered to it, "I won't be able to feel you in my hand ever again."

That thought lingered in his mind for a long moment. The day was coming fast where he wouldn't have feelings in his hands anymore. And one day he'll lose his eyesight, and his sense of taste. All his five senses gone, just like that. That finality slapped him hard emotionally, as well as intellectually, until, after thinking about it some more, he clicked open his pen and wrote in bold letters at the top of the paper: "My Best Five," and then underlined it.

He sat back and began to think, staring at those words, but nothing was coming to him, so he stood, slipped the baseball mitt on his hand again and began to toss the ball. A moment passed. Still nothing came to him. He moved over to the bed and lied down. He tossed the ball up in the air and caught it several times, still thinking. After about ten minutes of this, suddenly an idea came to him. He got up, went back to the desk and began to make his list.

CHAPTER TEN

THE NEXT MORNING, APRIL WAS in the kitchen preparing breakfast. Raine entered the room holding the sheet of paper he had worked on late into the night. He made his way over to his sister with a slight grin on his face. April looked at him suspiciously when he tried to lean in and kiss her. She quickly pulled away.

"What are you doing?" she asked, bothered.

"I was going to kiss your cheek," Raine said, innocently.

"Why?" April asked in a tone that made it clear she wasn't interested in any answer he had to give.

Raine took a step back, rejected and feeling stupid. April, suddenly overcome with a surge of forgiveness and regret, tearfully grabbed her brother and hugged him tight.

"I'm sorry. I'm so sorry about last night," she moaned into his shoulder.

Raine hugged her back, feeling the same. "Me, too. It's OK," he whispered.

As he tried to gently pull away, April tightened her grip. Raine allowed the moment to last just several seconds more before trying to gently pull away again, but April wasn't letting him go.

Raine winced in awkward discomfort and said, "Uh – you think I can get some coffee?"

April gradually pulled away, wiped her tears and grabbed two mugs from a cabinet as Raine took a seat at the table. She poured the coffee, and then took a seat across from him. Raine took a sip eyeing her carefully.

"You kicked my ass last night," he said with a slight chuckle.

"I said I was sorry," April replied, her voice cracking once again with deep regret.

"Don't be," said Raine, as he placed his mug on the table. "I needed it. You gave me a lot to think about. I couldn't sleep."

April lowered her head, feeling terrible. "I'm sorry," she said again, ready to let loose a wave of tears.

"No, no," said Raine quickly, hoping to avoid the flood. "It was good because I've decided to go away for a while."

April looked up, confused. "What?"

"For just a little while," said Raine, wanting to calm any worry.

"What's a little while? A day? Raine, it's not a good time for you to go anywhere."

Raine saw that just the thought of his leaving was beginning to cause his sister anxiety, as well as anger, so he did his best to ease some of her concern.

"I thought long and hard about this. It's something I

need to do. Look, I made a list and want to complete everything on it before…you know."

"You made a bucket list?"

"Not exactly. It's a list of my best five."

April looked at him perplexed.

"Remember when you said I always say everything is "the best"? Well, I thought about that and made a list of my best five, one for each of my senses. Before I lose them, I want to relive the best thing I'd ever seen, the best thing I've ever touched.   The best thing I've ever tasted…smelled, heard."

"And you wrote all of this down?" asked April sounding annoyed, but a little intrigued.

"Yeah," answered Raine as he handed the list to her. April looked at it carefully, and then shook her head in disgust.

"Really, Raine? The best things you've ever seen in your life were Louise Gardner's legs?"

"They were awesome," Raine responded without hesitation, sounding like a fourteen year-old schoolboy.

"Not the Grand Canyon, or the Mona Lisa?" asked April, as if trying to mature her brother in a matter of seconds, and in hopes to continue a more tolerable conversation.

"I've never seen the Grand Canyon, or the Mona Lisa, but I've seen this girl's legs and I'm telling you, they were the best! I want to see them again. Is that too much to ask from someone in my condition?"

"Who is she?

"I met her when I spent that summer in Rhode Island. She was bartending at this place I used to hang out at."

April rolled her eyes. "So, you're going to go back to a bar, find this girl and say, 'Hi, I'm dying...can I see your legs?'"

"Not like that," said Raine, shooting her a look of aversion at her insensitivity. "I'll be more...subtle. And I'm not going to say I'm dying. I don't want anyone to feel sorry for me. I want it to come out...naturally. Organic. I want to recreate each one of these as close to the first time it happened as possible." He grinned proudly at his idea.

April stared at him with part scowl, part disbelief. Raine noticed.

"I'll never get the chance to have it again, April," Raine argued. "You go through life thinking that it's forever...well, it's not. And at least I know how much time I got, give or take a week, with the chance to, you know, make something of it. Not like some poor schmuck who will cross a street today and get hit by a bus. No, I'm taking what time I have left and doing something I want to do, not sit in my room being bitter and angry."

April gently began to cry.

"Oh, jeez, why are you crying?" asked Raine in a tired tone.

"I took time off work so I could take care of you and...really get to know you," she answered.

Raine responded softly and sincerely, "You know me, April."

"But there's so little time," she said between small, stabbing sobs.

"Exactly," Raine said, keeping his tone level and assuring. "Let me do this. Otherwise, I'll stay here and we'll only get on each other's nerves. And there will be more blowouts like last night. That's not how I want you to remember me. I hate the thought of coming back here and being a burden to you, especially when I do start to lose all of my senses."

"But your condition...the medications..." April said sounding confused and distraught.

"Fuck them," said Raine as he reached over and grabbed April's hand. "It's only for a little while. All these places are nearby. I can easily drive to them."

April looked at him, even more worried.

"I want to do this. I have to do this. It's all I have left, literally. What have I got to lose?"

April looked at her brother. Who was she to stand in his way? She knew he was right, and slowly pulled her hand away to reach for a Kleenex. "I think you've lost your mind already," she said sarcastically before blowing her nose.

"Well, they say it's the first to go, so – "

April chuckled. So did Raine. It was a relief from such an otherwise gloomy conversation. April looked again at her brother's list and let out a heavy, resigning sigh. She put on an understanding, yet still sad face, slid the paper across the table. "Just stay in touch with me. And promise you'll come back the first sign of...anything."

Raine smiled and nodded. "I promise."

CHAPTER ELEVEN

THE NEXT DAY, APRIL STOOD on the front porch with Guy and waved goodbye to her brother as he pulled out of the driveway. He drove an old model Lexus that once belonged to his father. The car was sitting in the garage, barely used, since his death. Once Raine drove out of sight, April leaned into Guy, resting her head on his chest, looking forlorn. She felt like crying, but no tears came. Guy wrapped his arms around her and gently led her back inside the house.

For Raine, it felt free being in a car. Driving was a freedom he always enjoyed, but being alone was something he cherished much more. It was nice being away from his sister's sad face, a constant reminder of his condition that he needed desperately to get away from. He didn't realize this fully until it was gone from his sight.

He loved the wind on his face and the speed and control of the car. It neither concerned nor frightened him that driving in his condition might be a reckless and dangerous thing to do. He scoffed when April mentioned it several times, and ignored Guy's offer to do the driving for him. He wasn't going to spend his last remaining days, or weeks, not making the most of them his way.

Raine couldn't help but put more pressure on the car's accelerator as he tore down the highway. He grinned when, after a couple of hours, the Connecticut road signs eventually dissolved into new ones welcoming him to Rhode Island. Being out of his home state made it feel as if he was leaving everything behind, including his illness. He felt a sense of nervous excitement when he turned off the highway after passing a sign for Providence, Rhode Island.

•••••

It was the afternoon by the time Raine reached his hotel and checked in. He stood at the front desk of the semi-posh hotel with his overnight bag at his feet and his laptop placed on the marble countertop. The front desk clerk, a young man who spoke in clipped politeness, greeted Raine with a sincere smile.

"Hi," Raine said without smiling back, "Reservation for Addison."

The clerk began punching in the letters on his computer even before Raine got to the "son" part of his name. "Yes. The Presidential Suite," said the clerk as he punched something else into the computer, then politely handed Raine a keycard.

"It's room 1204, on the 12th floor. The elevators are to your right."

Raine took the keycard and tucked his laptop under his arm. As he reached for his overnight bag, he said to the clerk, "I have a few documents to print out later. Is there a printer?"

"Yes. The concierge will be able to help you with that," he said, still smiling.

"Thanks," said Raine as he grabbed his bag and headed for the elevator.

The ride to the twelfth floor was short, but lonely. Raine was the only one in the elevator. There was no wind blowing through his hair, or a motor growling beneath him, only the hum of the elevator mixed with the bland instrumental music. This depressed him, and all he wanted was to get to his room fast. When the elevator doors opened, he stepped out quickly and found his room without a problem, almost without even looking, as if he knew where it would be and simply approached the door, swiped the keycard and entered.

Once inside, Raine tossed his bag and laptop on the queen sized bed. It was an extremely large suite for one person, he thought, but he was dying, so why not have the biggest and the best? He quickly grabbed his laptop and placed it on a nearby table that was next to a window. He opened the laptop, turned it on, and then pulled out a chair and sat down. He opened a fresh Word document, preparing to compose his thoughts, and then removed his list from his pocket. He unfolded and studied it.

As he held it in his hand, he looked out the window and began to think. His eyes focused on the sky outside. The clouds were thick and snowy white, and the sky was a perfect blue. It had been years since he stopped and appreciated the magnificence and vastness of what hung above him all his life. The same way he watched it while sitting on April's porch. He thought of how it was so simple, yet so grand.

Raine wondered why he hadn't paid much attention to the sky most of his life. Maybe because it was just always there, and always would be, that was until he realized that he wouldn't be. It was an odd thought to think that one day he would be gone, but the sky would still remain. He didn't know how to process that concept, and it bothered him, but he had more important things to think about, so he looked back at his list, and then the computer screen. He stared at it for a long while before he began to type.

CHAPTER TWELVE

IT WAS LATE AFTERNOON BY the time Raine finished composing most of his thoughts. He closed down his laptop and got ready for his meeting with Louise Gardner. Of course, there was no guarantee that she would be there. It was, after all, years since he'd been in Providence, let alone in contact with his former flame. He thought about calling the bar to see if she still worked there, but decided against it since he wanted to see the place one last time anyway. Plus, if she was there, he wanted to speak with her in person and not over the phone.

He decided to dress comfortably, but still wanted to reek of success. This was not a conscious idea, just something that over time came naturally to Raine. In his mind he was success, and easily forgot that he was dying as he slipped into his five thousand dollar leather jacket made by Balmian.

Raine casually roamed the streets, enjoying the familiar surroundings before he found the place he was looking for. He walked into the Thesis Bar and Grill with ease and confidence. It was a local restaurant/bar filled mostly with college students and young professionals. He knew this establishment well since it was the number one hangout for him and his buddies many years earlier. It looked pretty much the same since he'd last been inside, maybe it had a fresh coat of paint and newer, nicer tablecloths, but outside of that not much had changed.

Raine's face registered warm recognition as he approached the bar wearing a smile. A young bartender eagerly walked over to him.

"What can I get you?" he asked.

"Hi," said Raine. "Actually, I'm looking for a girl."

The bartender grinned. "Aren't we all?"

Raine chuckled. "She was a bartender here a while back. I used to date her."

"How far back are we talking?" asked the bartender.

Raine winced when he gave his answer. "About ten years."

"Whoa, that's going back a ways. What's her name?"

"Louise Gardner."

"Louise Gardner," repeated the bartender. "Don't know her, sorry."

Raine sighed. He knew it was a long shot. He never bothered to learn much more about this girl when he was dating her, and didn't have much more information to give to the bartender on how to find her. Even the word "dating" was too serious a word for what they actually were to each other. Or, what she was to him, he now realized, and felt a sudden sense of shame for even being there and asking for her after all this time.

"Hey! Hold on a sec," said the bartender. "Let me ask Don. He was the manager back then. He might know where she is."

As he scuttled down the bar, flipped up the wooden flap to get out from behind it and disappeared into a back room, Raine felt a surge of excitement, yet at the same time, dread. He wanted to find Louise...but did he really? Was this a bad idea or a good one? Should he quickly turn and head for the door? Those questions raced through his head, and he knew he only had a short time to answer them honestly.

Deciding to leave, he reached into his pocket to pull out some bills to leave for the bartender, but instead he pulled out his list. He paused when he saw it, and then slowly unfolded and stared at it. It was weird seeing that list in a place where he was once something so different. Suddenly, he wasn't the healthy, good-looking Wall Street hopeful anymore. Instead, he was a guy dying from a brain tumor who was looking to relive just a few brief moments of his past before he…

"Are you looking for Louise Gardner?" a voice called out to Raine.

Raine quickly looked up. Approaching him was a portly, friendly looking man in his late fifties. He wore a crew cut and a shirt that badly needed ironing. The first four buttons were open, exposing the stubby, greying chest hair that matched the ones on his head.

"Yes," said Raine, quickly folding up his list and shoving it back in his pocket.

"She doesn't work here anymore. That was a long

time ago."

"Do you remember her?" asked Raine.

The portly man smiled. "I hired her. Yeah. Sweet girl."

"Do you know where I can reach her?" Raine asked, still unsure if he had any real intention of contacting her.

"Yeah. I have an address," said the portly man. "Hang on."

He waddled down to the other end of the bar and grabbed a pen and a napkin. He took a card from his pocket and copied down what was on the card on to the napkin, and then waddled back toward Raine.

"Here ya go," said the portly man as he handed Raine the napkin. "I don't think she'd mind me giving it to you."

Raine took the napkin and said meekly, "I used to date her."

"You used to date her?" he asked, sounding surprised.

"Yeah," Raine said with a chuckle. "Way back in the day."

"No kidding," said the portly man with a grin. "Well, good luck to ya."

"Thanks," said Raine as he held up the napkin. "I appreciate it." Raine then turned and walked out of the Thesis Bar and Grill for the last time.

•••••

Raine sat in his car for the longest time staring at the address on the napkin. It wasn't as if he was having second thoughts. No, he was ready to follow through with what he started, but he didn't know how, or what to say, once he did come face to face with Louise again. Their time together didn't end badly, not from what he remembered, but what does one say to someone they were once so intimate with and well over ten years ago?

Intimate, that was a funny word, Raine thought. When was he ever intimate with anyone? But he was intimate with Louise, in that way, he reasoned, and it was enough to at least say hello to him. Or was it?

Raine knew that if he sat there for much longer he would change his mind and drive back to Connecticut to sit out his last days with a weeping sister. But since that was not an option, he started the car and pulled out of the parking lot to find his former whatever you want to call her.

Raine easily found the area where Louise was living, but not the exact address. He drove in circles in search for the number that was on the napkin. After doing this for nearly fifteen minutes, he finally pulled over and decided to search on foot. He wandered up and down the block, carefully reading the numbers aloud to himself. After counting the numbers on the homes and buildings, he found a large wooden door that was hidden by overgrown ivy. It was the only entrance to a large, stone building. There was no number on the door, but all the other numbers on the street matched the other buildings. Puzzled, Raine stepped up to the thick wooden door anyway and pulled on the thin rope that rang a tiny bell above the door. Was anyone going to hear that thing? He wondered.

A moment later, the sound of the wooden door's latch being lifted was heard from behind it. Raine took a step back, not knowing what to expect. As the door slowly opened, Raine's expression went from apprehension to utter confusion when he saw an elderly nun standing there.

"Yes?" she asked, wearing the most serene smile Raine had ever seen.

Thrown, Raine stumbled with his words. "Uh, hi. I, uh…I'm looking for Louise Gardner. I'm an old friend?"

Raine felt stupid saying "old friend" as if it were a question. Probably because he didn't know what else to call his connection to Louise, especially in front of a nun, but more because he felt dirty knowing exactly what his connect to Louise was.

The nun smiled. "Yes. She's here," she replied.

Just then, Louise Gardner appeared behind the nun. She was stunningly attractive with a warm, open smile, and dressed in full nun habit from head to toe.

"Raine?" she asked, pleased and surprised to see him.

Raine stared at her in utter shock. "Louise?"

The elderly nun stepped aside and walked away as Louise stepped forward.

"Yes! Hi. What are you doing here?" she asked, letting out a slight giggle.

"I-I went to the bar…the one you used to…where we…" Raine stammered.

Louise let out a laugh. "I don't work there anymore. Obviously."

"Right. No. Yeah. Of course," said Raine, fumbling.

"Were you looking for me?" Louise asked sweetly.

"Well, yeah. I was in town and I was thinking of

you, and thought...I thought..." Raine stammered again.

Remembering why he was there made him look away. He was there to see her legs, but now...oh, God, this was awkward, he thought. God? Did he really just bring God into this? He suddenly felt like a pervert, and quickly blurted out, "I just wanted to say hi." Then, trying to hide his obvious discomfort followed it with, "Wow. You're a nun now."

Seeing his struggle, Louise stepped outside and closed the wooden door behind her. "Let's go for a walk," she said as she gently took his arm and led him around the stone building and down a narrow path that opened up to a small yet beautiful, tranquil garden that sat behind the nunnery.

As they slowly paced the grounds, and after they answered the customary "how are you?" type questions, Raine asked how she became a nun of all things.

"I was going to college, as you know, to study psychology..."

"You were a psychology major?" Raine asked, surprised.

Louise looked at him, puzzled. He didn't know this? She let it pass and continued, "I thought I wanted to be a therapist, but realized I wasn't here to 'fix' people. Instead, I was here to help them find a better path."

"Yeah...OK," said Raine, trying to understand. "But now you're a...and, you and me...we did things." He lowered his voice to a whisper. "Together. Alone. In the dark. A lot."

Louise laughed. "You don't have to whisper, Raine. The nuns know about my past. So does God, so there's nothing to hide. And, yes, we did do a lot of things in the dark, but I am celibate now. That part of my life is far behind me."

Raine looked at her and shook his head. What a waste, he thought.

Louise knew what he was thinking because she'd gotten that reaction so many times before, and laughed. "So, enough about me. What about you? What are you in town for?"

Raine felt caught by the question. He obviously couldn't tell her now why he was really there, so he chuckled nervously and said, "Business. Just business."

"I take it you're a financial hotshot now? That was always your goal. Your very laser-focused goal, as I recall."

"Yeah. I am," said Raine. He looked away, suddenly embarrassed by it.

"You know, the last time we were together, you told me you were moving to New York to…wait, how did you put it? 'To be bigger than Donald Trump, and date Charlize Theron'."

Raine winced. "Did I really say that to you?" he asked, embarrassed.

Louise nodded yes.

"What a douche bag," Raine whispered under his breath.

"Yes, you were. I actually thought we'd get married, but obviously you had other things you wanted. And, it turned out, so did I."

Raine felt like a heel. She had actually thought that much of him to want to marry him back then? It never once entered his mind, nor was he even remotely aware, of anything she might have wanted. He couldn't believe how incredibly selfish he had been. "I'm sorry," Raine said to her with deep sincerity.

Louise laughed. "Oh, don't be. God has His plan for us. It's rarely the same as ours."

Raine looked at her, impressed by her easy forgiveness and peaceful demeanor. They spent another thirty minutes or so talking about the past and about April. Raine was surprised when Louise asked about her since they had never met, but Louise remembered he mentioned many times his "artist sister back home" when they were together, and she was genuinely interested in how her life turned out. Raine mentioned she was marrying a fireman, and that made Louise smile. As they approached back to the path that led out of the garden, they both stopped.

"I'm glad you came by to see me, Raine. It was so good to see you again."

"Yeah," said Raine, weakly. He looked down at the ground, not wanting to leave.

Knowing him so well, Louise picked up on this. "Is there another reason why you came to see me?"

Raine looked up at her. Yes, there was. He was dying and wanted to tell her. He also wanted to tell her about his list, and how he was going to lose his eyesight one day soon and wanted to take one last look at her beautiful legs, but he couldn't. Not now, especially not with that cross dangling delicately on her chest. He glanced at it, and then quickly looked away, feeling again like a degenerate.

"God," he whispered in defeat.

"He's listening," said Louise softly.

"That's what I'm afraid of," said Raine, worried.

Louise let out a cheerful laugh, stepped forward and gave him a warm embrace. Raine hugged her back, holding her tight, knowing this would be the last time he'd ever see her. He felt like crying. It was safe in her arms and he wanted to stay there forever.

Why hadn't he been more present like this when he was with her, and had her, all those years ago? This wonderful, gentle woman who was now giving him complete unconditional love and acceptance. He let out a deep sigh, and allowed himself to feel the profound sense of loss of "what might have been."

Louise could feel his longing, so she whispered softly into his ear, "It's God's plan. And it is good."

With that, she gently pulled away, turned and walked back into the garden. Raine watched her go toward another wooden door near the back that led into the stone encased nunnery. She opened it, turned and gave Raine one last wave. He waved back. She entered, and closed the door for good.

Raine lingered in the garden for a little while longer. It was hard to leave such a beautiful spot, one where he felt such peace. He couldn't recall the last time he felt that sort of serenity, or even if he had ever felt it at all.

CHAPTER THIRTEEN

WHEN RAINE RETURNED TO HIS hotel suite, he sat by the window again and stared out at the sky. His time with Louise made him think about missed opportunities. Not just with her, but with so many others. After about an hour of reflection, he was on his cell phone with April, telling her about his failed mission.

"She's a nun," he said, shaking his head in defeat, and then waited for April's laughter to die down. "Yeah, ha-ha, funny. I guess this wasn't such a good idea after all. I don't know what made me think it would be easy," he said rubbing his forehead.

He listened carefully as April encouraged him to keep going, surprised by her change of heart. She explained that after having thought about it, and talked it over with Guy, she realized that Raine needed to do something to help him through this trying time, even if it meant getting one last peek at a woman's legs. But Raine was too tired to agree.

"No, I'm done. I'll start back in the morning. Yeah, I'll be OK. I've had worse ideas in my life. I'll see you tomorrow," he said, and then hung up.

Raine took the list from his pocket and looked at it again before crumbling it up and lying down on the bed. He curled up, faced the window, and looked out at the sky again. He did this for a long while, thinking about Louise and where else he had failed in his life before his eyes drooped and closed.

His sleep was hard and long. The tumor caused this. In the past, he could easily go with only four hours of sleep. Now, when he slept, it was deep and sound.

It was many hours later that Raine awoke to the sound of a knock on his hotel door. He slowly opened his eyes, and since the room was dark, he, at first, had no idea where he was. This frightened him for a few seconds. Am I dead? He wondered before noticing the glow outside the window from the city lights below.

Relieved, he sat up and noticed he was still in his clothes from earlier that day. The knock on the door again made him get up and quickly turn on the light. He ran his hand through his hair and tried to look alert as he went to answer it. It was probably room service, he thought. Maybe he ordered something before falling asleep, but he couldn't remember.

When he opened the door, he was shocked to find Louise Gardner standing there wearing that warm, inviting smile.

"Louise! What are you doing here?" asked Raine, confused and dazed.

"Why didn't you tell me you were dying?" she

asked, her smile fading to serious concern.

Raine looked at her surprised and perplexed. How did she know? He wondered.

"Your sister phoned and told me," she answered before he could ask.

Raine turned and walked back in the room. He didn't know whether to be angry with April or thank her. Either way, being found half asleep and in rumpled clothing, looking like a depressed bum was embarrassing. He also hated pity of any kind. He especially didn't want it from Louise, a woman he used to fuck who was now a nun. Could his life get any more pathetic?

"I didn't want anyone to know," Raine said in a gruff way, though he was trying to sound polite.

"You wanted people to find out after you were gone?" asked Louise, confused, but sympathetic as she followed him. "Not give anyone the chance to say what they want or need to say to you?"

"I don't think I want to hear what they want or need to say," responded Raine, hinting that she wasn't the only one he'd hurt in the past.

"Raine," Louise began, "We all do things that hurt people. Sometimes deliberately, sometimes not, but you'd be surprised how forgiving most people are."

"Only because I'm dying," Raine said, hating to admit this.

"Maybe. But maybe it helps them clear their conscience just as you'd want to clear yours."

Raine made his way across the room and sat in the semi-darkness near the window. He rubbed his face with his hands, and then stared down at the floor. "Maybe I don't deserve it."

"Oh, deserving. Yes. It's what most people struggle with. I hear it all the time," said Louise, softly.

Raine looked up at her, interested.

"You know, for the longest time I felt I didn't deserve you," she said. "You were this handsome, strong, smart guy that could have any woman he wanted...and you probably did."

Raine shamefully nodded.

Louise chuckled. "And somewhere deep inside of me I knew that, but still...you were with me, and I struggled with that deep sense of not deserving you. But then, one night, after we made love and you were sleeping, I lied awake and watched you, and it occurred to me that I did deserve you. Actually, the problem had nothing to do with deserving, which I now believe there is no such thing. The problem was with allowing. I wasn't allowing myself to be with you, but got over that. I did finally allow myself to have you, Raine. It was you who didn't allow yourself to have me. Yes, you could make love to my body and say all the right things to make me feel special. You could even climb to the top of any financial institution and make yourself millions of dollars, but you could never allow yourself to really feel and enjoy it. That's where you got tripped up. That's where everyone gets tripped up. Everyone is deserving, but not everyone allows themselves to enjoy what they have...or what they could have."

Raine looked away, contemplating every word she said. She was right. He never allowed himself much of anything. Not with any of the money, women and success. He had it all, but the reality was he had nothing. He couldn't even remember the last time he felt real joy or happiness.

Louise took several steps toward him and asked, "So…are my legs really the best thing you've ever seen?"

Raine was gob smacked. He shot a startled, embarrassed look at Louise, and then quickly looked away. "I can't believe my sister told you that," he said, wanting to strangle April.

Louise smiled and let out a soft giggle. "She told me because she loves you, and knows how important it is to you."

"God, this is so embarrassing," said Raine shaking his head and covering his face with his hands.

Louise giggled again. "He knows," she said.

"Man, is there anything God doesn't know?" Raine groaned in humiliation.

Louise took a few more steps toward him. "So…are they?" she asked referring to her legs.

Raine pulled his hands away from his face, looked at her and suddenly felt his confidence kicking in. "Yeah. They are. You were gorgeous."

"And I'm not anymore?" she asked.

Raine looked at her confused. Where was this going? He wondered. "Well, no…I mean, yes, you still are, but…" he said pointing to her clothing.

Louise looked down at her nun robe. "Yes. It's not a mini skirt and heels, I'll agree," she said. "But I'm still the same person inside." She then looked at him sincerely. "Raine, I've given up what I used to do. Serving God is a lot more rewarding to me then serving beer." She then went over to a chair next to Raine, sat down, and took his hands into hers. "I know what you're facing is difficult. And knowing you, you're angry about it."

Raine nodded. "Yeah. I'm pissed."

"And you're also scared."

Raine nodded again. There was no use pretending with her any longer.

"And who wouldn't be?" she asked. "I know you're not a religious guy, but if you need comfort, please don't turn your back on God. And if you need to talk, I want you to know that I'm here for you. I will be praying."

Raine, surprised by her kindness, looked into her eyes. They were clear and comforting, and he knew she meant every word. It was so foreign for him to feel so much trust. He had never experienced it before in his life. The thought briefly crossed his mind to kiss her, but not because he wanted her in that way, but to thank her. He didn't kiss her, for fear of any misinterpretations, but somehow knew that she knew all of his thoughts and understood.

"Thank you," Raine said with deep sincerity.

Louise smiled and stood. As she began to make her way toward the door, she stopped and turned to face him.

"As I was training to become a nun, I had a lot of struggles," she said softly. "I had a lot of questions, but gradually, I just began to trust, and soon, my questions didn't matter anymore. All that did was my faith. And it's true to me that God has a plan, and all I can do is follow it as it unfolds and presents itself, so…"

She gently took hold of the edges of her long, black robe and began to raise it up.

Raine quickly stood. "Wait...what are you doing?"

he asked, urgently.

"A dying man's last request," she said as she continued to raise the robe. "There can be no harm in allowing you to see one last time what you consider your best. Just allow it, Raine."

And with that, she raised her robe, giving Raine full view of her stunning legs. They were gorgeously long and flawless, just as he had remembered them. Raine stared, surprised that he didn't at all feel like a pervert, nor was he filled with lust. Her legs were truly beautiful, like two sculptures created by Michelangelo, and he felt grateful for the chance to see them just one more time.

"Thank you," he whispered as tears filled his eyes.

Louise then slowly lowered her robe. She walked over to Raine, touched his face as she stared into his eyes, and offered him a warm, loving smile. This gave Raine an intense feeling of belonging and acceptance that he had never had before which cause several tears to fall down his cheeks.

With nothing left to say, Louise quietly turned, went to the door and walked out of Raine's life for the last time.

CHAPTER FOURTEEN

AFTER LOUISE LEFT, RAINE SPENT several hours working on his laptop. He then called the front desk to have what he had written printed and ready for him in the morning. Once that was done, he sat by the window and contemplated his last moments with Louise, feeling an indescribable sense of freedom.

Staring out the window and up at the darkened sky, he thought about how lucky he was. The brain tumor was something he had, and he understood it was fatal, but that didn't concern him that evening. He was alive and felt fortunate. Feeling in harmony with the sky was all that mattered. And that's how he continued to feel when he finally climbed into bed and turned out the light. It guaranteed him a much-needed, full night, tranquil sleep, which he hadn't had in a very long time.

The next morning, Raine awoke early. He found himself humming a long forgotten 1990's tune as he showered and got dressed. He was able to recall what the song was about, but none of its words, and chuckled when he tried to remember them. It didn't matter, he thought, as long as he got the melody right. He grabbed his overnight bag, laptop and the crumpled list that he had on the nightstand and left the room, wearing a renewed look of determination on his face.

Raine collected the several sheets of paper he had printed out the night before from the clerk at the front desk, and stuffed each printed page into an envelope as the clerk checked him out. With everything complete, Raine signed the bill, thanked the clerk for the use of the printer, shoved the envelopes into his overnight bag, grabbed his laptop and left.

Once he was inside the Lexus, he pulled out his cell phone and punched in a number that he had written on the back of a sheet of the hotel's stationary. A number he had looked up on Google and collected earlier that morning.

"Yeah, hi," Raine said, speaking politely into the phone. "I'm a former graduate, the name is Raine Addison. I'm trying to track down another alumni. We lived in the same dorm. The name is George Doit. He's from New Jersey. We both graduated in 2004. I'd like to get his current address. Addison. Yes, I'll hold."

As Raine waited, he reached into his overnight bag and pulled out a pen. He tapped the steering wheel with it until someone came back on the phone. He listened carefully to what the person had to say, which changed his politeness into curt resentment.

"Look, if you can't give me a simple address, then explain to me exactly what I get for the fat check I write out to your alumni every year? And while you're explaining, you may want to type my name into your computer's financial records and see how much I've given back. It's in the six figures," he said with authority, and then added, "We have two ways this can go down...you either make this easy by giving me the address now, or I'll call my office and have someone there get it for me, and from now on I will write all my future checks to Princeton and Harvard, which will it be? Yeah, I'll hold."

Raine didn't like threatening the young kid on the other end of the phone. He understood the kid was just doing his job, but all he wanted was a stupid address. He let out a sigh as he waited, and thought about the address he was trying to get. It belonged to his friend, George Doit.

What a great last name, he thought. Doit. Do-it. He wished he had a name like that. It made people smile when they heard it, unlike his name. He was tired of having to explain how his parents came up with the name "Raine," and even more tired of saying "with an 'e' at the end". He also hated when people asked, "As in the weather?" Raine let out another frustrated sigh just thinking about it.

After several minutes, the kid came back on the line and asked if Raine had a pen. Raine grinned as he wrote down the address, and thanked the kid on the other end before he hung up.

"Money talks," he muttered as he tossed the pen on the top of his bag, looked at the address and started the car. "Going to New Jersey," he said aloud as he pulled out of the hotel parking lot and got on the road.

It was a little over a three-hour drive from Providence to Little Ferry, New Jersey. Raine killed most of the time listening to a radio station that played hits from the 1990's and after. The music brought back memories of his younger days as a kid, growing up in Connecticut with April and his parents. He reminisced about going through elementary school, junior high, and then high school. He laughed at how the songs were like a playlist of his life. Most of the songs reminded him of college. Nights filled with drinking, getting laid and studying... usually in that order. He loved college. He laughed when a song came on that triggered memories of eating crappy food in the cafeteria. Any song by the Foo Fighters reminded him of that. Anything by John Mayer on low volume always reminded him of whispering lies into some sophomore girl's ear as he undressed her.

He easily forgot his condition when he listened to these songs. Every one of them was like a flash card to a specific time when he was healthy and strong. He recalled classes that he hated and professors that he liked. Football games in the fall when he sat on cold bleachers, screaming angrily at the players on the field for a touchdown. Passing mid-term's, but struggling with finals. Smoking a lot of pot while arguing conspiracy theories about 9/11 and the Kennedy assassination with his buddies. Music and songs brought all of this back, and for three blissful hours on the road, he was young again.

Raine was ready to get out of the car when he pulled into the driveway of his old friend's three-bedroom home. His legs badly needed stretching. He looked at the house as he closed the car door, noticing that it was a bit rundown. The harsh winters and age was the cause of that. Although he knew his dorm mate George Doit well, he had never visited his home. School was where the relationship began and ended. For holidays and summers everyone went back to wherever they came from and returned once the break was over. Just knowing the name of the state or town where someone was from was enough. Still, Raine found himself wishing he had visited his friend at least once, so his "dropping by" didn't feel so damn awkward.

He walked cautiously up the several steps to the front door and rang the doorbell. Several moments passed until he heard footsteps approach from the inside. The lock unlatched and the door opened. Standing there was a woman in her sixties with greying hair. She was plump, and had a weary yet welcoming air about her.

"Hi," said Raine with a smile. "I was wondering if George Doit still lived here? My name is Raine Addison. We went to college together. We lived in the same dorm."

The woman's face lit up when she heard this. "Raine Addison?" she asked in surprise recognition. "Oh, yes! My son told me about you. I'm his mother. I remember you because of the name. Raine. Like in the weather." She held opened the door. "Come in! Come in!"

Raine didn't want to go inside. The house seemed void and hollow in spirit, though filled with the typical things one would find in a house belonging to a tired, suburban woman of her age. But Raine obliged and stepped inside. He lingered near the front door as George's mother slowly turned and made her way into her living room. Raine hesitated in following her, but eventually he did. He glanced at the old furniture, probably from the 1970's, as well as the vases and cheap candles placed upon them. He just wanted to know where George was, not have to sit alone with this stranger who would probably at any minute offer him tea. He made a promise to himself to say no if she did.

"Can I get you some tea?" she asked.

"Sure," answered Raine, kicking himself soon after for giving the wrong answer.

"Let's go in the kitchen," she said in a gracious way as she moved lazily further back into the house where the kitchen was.

Raine followed. "I hope I'm not interrupting your day," he said just out of politeness. It was obvious that he wasn't.

"Oh, no. I'm not doing anything," said George's mother when she turned her head and gave him a happy smile. She entered the kitchen and went right for the teakettle that was sitting lopsided on top of the stove. "Please, have a seat," she semi-shouted over the splashing water from the sink's tap that she was filling the kettle with.

Raine sat at one end of a small, wooden, colonial style table that had a thick, engraved base. It was ugly, but Raine kept that to himself.

"So, you're George's mother," he said, trying to fill the awkward silence that fell between them while she was taking down cups from a shelf and pulling tea bags from a Lipton box.

"Yes. Oh, George will be so glad to know you stopped by."

"He's not here?" Raine asked, and then quickly wondered how to get out of there. This woman was lonely, and if he didn't come up with a plan fast, he might be stuck there until nightfall.

"No. He's…not here," she said sadly as she busied herself with finding spoons in a drawer.

"Does he live in town?" Raine asked, hopeful.

"No," she answered, bringing the spoons and cups to the table. "It's been eight years now since he's been home. His room is still upstairs though, ready for him when he does."

Great, Raine thought, this woman wasn't going to just tell him where George was and be done with it. He had to ask the questions, the right ones, and politely, until he had his answer.

"Where is he?" Raine asked, hoping that would win him the jackpot.

George's mother didn't answer right away. She was more interested in getting the tea on the table. The kettle began to let out a shrieking whistle, which she quickly stifled by taking it off its burner. She carried it over to the table and carefully poured the boiling water into both cups. Raine watched the teabags float to the top of the cups as she did this. He also watched with impatience as she slowly went back to the stove, placed the kettle down and returned to the table, taking a seat uncomfortably close to Raine.

"Here's the sugar," she said moving a small, white covered bowl from the center of the table toward Raine. "And here's cream from this morning. It's still fresh," she added pushing a matching small, white pouring cup in his direction.

"I'll have it straight," Raine said, as he tied his teabag around his spoon, pressed hard to drain it with his thumb and set it carefully on the table. After another moment of silence, Raine said, "So…" wearing a forced smile.

George's mother blew on her tea several times before she looked up. "You heard about George, right?" she asked in a way that made it obvious she didn't want to say.

Raine shook his head no, trying to hide his worry about what was coming next.

"Why do you want to see him?" George's mother asked, again, avoiding the questing by asking one of her own.

Raine didn't expect to have to tell her why. He really believed he would just stop by, find George, and then be on his way. But not knowing where George was, or why his mother was avoiding his simple questions, he began having a nagging feeling that something bad had happened to his old college friend, so he decided to simply tell her the truth…or, at least part of it.

"Well," Raine began, "back in college, I lived in the same dorm as George, on the same floor. He had a room down the hall from me. We used to…well; we were kind of wild back then, drinking and all that. Anyway, I know this is going to sound strange but, George had the best laugh I'd ever heard."

A huge smile formed across George's mother's face after Raine said this. "Oh, yes. That laugh! Everyone loved his laugh," she said, and then took a sip of her tea.

"It was the best," said Raine, now feeling relaxed having finally found a shared connection with this woman. "In fact, his laugh was the best sound I'd ever heard in my entire life."

George's mother let out a laugh herself upon

hearing this. It was similar to her son's, but not as boisterous and without that odd pitch that was distinctly George's. Her laugh set Raine at ease even more, to the degree that he began to share a story.

"I remember this one time…actually, no, I probably shouldn't tell you this," he said.

"Oh, please do," George's mother encouraged him. "I don't know much about his college years. He shared very little, and I'd like very much to know how he used to be."

She looked at Raine with sad, pleading eyes. They reminded him of April's. Through them, he understood the depth of April's complaint about remembering and sharing stories about someone who was no longer around, and how it was a need that only certain people could fulfill. But where was George? Why wasn't he around? He wondered. Raine paused for a moment taking this in, and then smiled. He no longer had any apprehensions about going into the crazy details of his story if it would make this poor woman's day.

"OK. Well, this one time in college, during midterms, it was pretty late and I had just taken a really hard exam. One way I liked to relax and unwind was to smoke weed. Everyone did, actually," he admitted.

George's mother nodded her head, with an understanding smile. She wasn't born yesterday.

"I, personally, only liked the good stuff, the expensive stuff, so I had just bought an ounce of the best shit...oh, jeez, pardon my expression," Raine said with a cringe.

George's mother smiled again and tapped his hand.

"It's all right. Go on," she said.

Raine smiled and continued. "Well, it cost me a lot of money. Anyway, I had just taken my last mid-term and was ready to kick back and enjoy myself. The stuff came right after I had gotten out of the shower. I was still dripping wet with just a towel around my waist when I saw my dealer standing at my door in the dorm. I let him in, gave him the cash, he gave me the weed and I was ready to light up. So ready that I didn't even bother to dress, or close my door. I stood at my desk, near my open window, and opened the bag to take a good whiff of it. As I did this, the RA happened by. He was a real prick...oops, sorry," said Raine, again, forgetting whom he was speaking to.

"It's all right," said George's mother, not caring and wanting to hear more.

"Anyway, I saw this...jerk...from the corner of my eye. He was the kind of guy that if he caught you doing anything, he would have you out of there in heartbeat. On instinct, and out of fear, I tossed the bag out the window.

"Oh, no," gasped George's mother.

"Oh, yeah," said Raine, liking that George's mother got the value of what went out that window.

"Well, the guy, the RA, didn't see me do any of that, he just passed my door. I stood there for a moment out of panic, I guess. Then, when I realized the guy wasn't coming back, I took off, out of my room, ran down the hall and out the front door to find my stash. Only thing was my towel fell off as I was halfway down the hall, which I didn't even realize. My mind on that bag of pot outside.

"Oh, no," said George's mother, covering her

mouth.

"Yeah. Thankfully, no one was around and saw me. Everyone was either out studying or taking mid-term's. So, I made my way outside of the building and climbed into the bushes that were directly below my window. My window faced the front of the building. It was early evening, so I couldn't see very well. I was rustling around naked in those bushes that had all this litter in there. Doritos bags, soda bottles, crap like that. I was feeling my way around the trash, and holding anything up to my face that felt like my bag of weed. Suddenly, who comes walking up? George. He had been in the library studying. He heard me in the bushes, took a closer look and saw that it me. 'What the hell are you doing?' he asked me. I told him to keep it down, and that I was looking for my bag of weed. He peered closer and said, 'Jeez, are you naked?' I told him I was and to stop looking so obvious. Just then, as my rotten luck would have it, two security cops come walking by. I was too busy scrounging around to notice, but they heard me in the bushes. George stood there in a panic, not knowing how to help me. The security cops stopped and looked into the bushes. One flashed a flashlight on me and told me to come out. I froze. It wasn't until that moment that I really felt naked, know what I mean?"

George's mother nodded her head, hanging on Raine's every word. "What did you do?" she asked.

"Like I said, I froze. I wasn't about to just walk out of the bushes naked, plus, what was I going to say I was doing in there? So, I just said, 'It's OK, I just lost something. I'll be out in a bit,' as if that would make them go away. They didn't. The one cop said, 'Come out now!' I looked at George and he looked not only nervous but also guilty, although he hadn't done anything. I was the naked guy in the bushes looking for pot, not him, but I think his expression is what raised the cops' suspicion. Anyway, by this time I'd forgotten about the pot and had to think fast about why I was naked in the bushes, but also, I didn't want to climb out with nothing on. So, I bent down and grabbed something to cover myself with. What I grabbed was a half roll of paper towel. Why it was back there, who knows, but it was the biggest thing I could find to cover myself up. But covering myself didn't seem like enough, so I…I…"

Raine hesitated. He realized at that point he had gone too far and didn't want to tell George's mother what he did. This wasn't an old college buddy he was sharing the with. This was George's mother. He felt like an idiot.

"What did you do?" she asked, dying to know.

"Oh, jeez…OK," Raine sighed. "I put my Johnson in the paper towel roll."

George's mother looked at him, puzzled at first, and then it registered. "Did it fit?" she asked, innocently.

"Did it…yes, it fit!" answered Raine with slight annoyance. "Anyway, I climbed out of the bushes wearing just this half full roll of paper towel on me. It looked like my cock was in a cast."

George's mother started to giggle, which slowly turned into full-out laughter. Her face became red and tears filled her eyes from laughing so hard. She had to hold her chest to steady herself. Raine began to laugh, too, as he finished the story.

"So, there I was with this thing between my legs. The cops jumped back as if they were going to get assaulted by it or something. And George, well, like you, he busted out laughing. But, you know that laugh of his, it was loud, boisterous and, well, you know…contagious. The cops started to laugh. And they laughed even harder when George fell to the ground, doubled-over with that loud laughing sound coming out of him. The cops were hanging on each other by this point, wiping their eyes. I couldn't tell anymore if they were laughing at me, or because of George."

George's mother continued to laugh, wiping her own eyes. Raine laughed, too. He was glad to have made this otherwise seemingly lonely woman regain a sense of life in her.

"Anyway, I lied to the cops and told them I had lost a bet and just wanted to get back to my room. Thankfully, they said OK and left. George was still on the ground laughing. I went over and kicked him with my foot. Not hard, but you know. He looked up, saw me standing over him with that paper towel roll still on me and busted up laughing again. I checked to see that the cops were gone, went back into the bushes, found my pot, and then we both went inside and smoked it."

George's mother took a napkin from the table and wiped her eyes. She let out short gasps of laughter as she composed herself. "Thank you for sharing that story with me. It's been so long since I had a good laugh," she said in all sincerity.

"I hope you don't judge me on that…it was a long time ago," Raine said.

"Oh, no. I don't judge you. And, sadly, yes. A long time ago," George's mother said. "I appreciate the story, and your honesty, as well as you wanting to see George. None of his friends come around anymore."

"What's going on with him?" Raine asked, hoping he'd finally get a direct answer.

"Well, he's not laughing much these days...in fact, not at all. He's in a hospital, Raine. He got off his addiction to heroin several years ago, but the use of the drug, and a lot of others, has done a lot of damage. He was in a coma a few times. Now he's just...he's not the same. He might be in there for the rest of his life."

Raine stared at George's mother, shocked and saddened. How could someone so happy and full of life, he wondered, end up like that? George's mother hung her head and wiped tears of sorrow from her eyes with the napkin.

Raine reached out and gently touched her hand. "Can I go see him anyway?"

"Would you?" she asked looking up into his eyes, as if that simple question, like his story that made her laugh, brought a sense of hope to her.

Raine nodded. He'd come all this way, he thought.

"Let me give you the address. It's about thirty or forty minutes from here in Morris Plains," she said as she rose from her chair and went to grab a business card that was on the refrigerator. She found a pencil and a piece of paper from the counter and began to carefully write the address on it. Raine watched as he took a small sip of tea from his cup. George's mother walked back over and handed him the paper.

"He never gets any visitors, except me, of course, so I'm not sure how he will respond to seeing you. If you want, I can call over there and tell them you're coming."

"No, I'd rather this be a surprise. That is, if he's OK with surprises," Raine said, looking concerned.

"Oh, he's not dangerous or anything, just sad and depressed. Clinically depressed. As I said, he's not what he used to be. Not as you knew him. He doesn't smile anymore, let alone laugh. I'm sorry," she said, as if it were her fault and, again, began tearing up.

"Hey, it's OK," said Raine, as he stood. He put his arm around her shoulder. "At least he's still with us, right?"

George's mother hugged Raine tight and began to sob. Raine was startled. Feeling compassion for the poor woman, he put both his arms around her and allowed her to cry. He wondered how long it had been since she even had a hug.

"I just want my boy happy," she said between sobs.

"I know…I know," said Raine as he held her tighter.

After a long moment of this, George's mother pulled away, regained her composure again and let out a tired laugh. "Thank you for coming. I really mean it."

"Thank you for having me here. And thanks for this," Raine said holding up the piece of paper. "Let's see if I can get him to smile."

"Oh, God, yes," said George's mother, holding her hands together as if in prayer. "But don't be too disappointed if he can't, Raine."

Raine nodded and they both walked to the front door. George's mother opened it, and Raine stepped out. She stepped out, too, to watch him leave. As Raine began heading down the steps, he stopped, went back up to

George's mother, leaned in and gave her a kiss on her cheek. This took her by surprise, and made her smile.

"Thank you," he said, and then hurried back down the steps to his car.

CHAPTER FIFTEEN

GEORGE'S MOTHER WAS RIGHT. IT was only about forty minutes from Little Ferry to Morris Plains. Though it was a short distance, it gave Raine enough time to think about George. He was greatly disturbed that such a happy guy could fall into a heroin addiction. How'd he get mixed up with that shit anyway? Raine wondered. Sure, they smoked a lot of pot in college, and drank, of course…even ate some mushrooms a couple of times, but heroin? That was the hard stuff, and everyone knew it was bad news.

George was such a fun-loving guy, Raine recalled, and could get rowdy like the rest of them, but nothing out of the ordinary. And he had a ton of friends. Raine couldn't think of anyone who had a bad thing to say about George…not ever, and felt guilty for not staying in touch.

Raine then thought about all the other guys in college he never stayed in touch with. He had lost touch with everyone. He was too focused on his career, of "making it" in the financial world. He had his eye on the prize once he finished school, and left everything all behind him. Staying in touch with that crowd was like yesterday's news to him. He felt like a heel.

He didn't once turn on the radio while in the car for fear of hearing an old song from those days. The memories now disturbed him. But, he wondered, where were all of George's other friends? The ones who stayed in touch? The addiction probably got so bad that they all kept their distance and fell away. Raine thought about how he probably would have done the same. How do you help a guy like that? Raine saw some of those shows on television about how out of control people with addictions got. He hated himself for thinking how lucky he was not to have been in touch with George during all that, but now here he was driving to Morris Plains, of all places, to visit him. And God only knew what was waiting for him.

Raine tried to focus only on the good times he had with his former friend. The guy who saved his ass a few times by helping him with his term papers, or pulling all-nighter's to make sure Raine passed his finals. George was that kind of guy. He was the guy that actually worried about how his friends were doing in school, and always asked how their classes were going. And George was always the guy to cover for friends when they were wasted and about to make total Asses out of themselves in front of a girl, or a visiting parent. In short, George was dependable and loyal.

And that laugh…God that laugh, Raine thought. He banged his fist on the steering wheel in anger when he thought how wonderful and life affirming it was, and how George was now, according to his mother, just a mere shadow of himself. What the hell happened? Raine regretted not asking his mother that question, but knew that he couldn't even if he had thought of it.

Raine pulled into the parking lot of the psychiatric hospital where his friend was residing. He parked and stared at the dismal surroundings. On the outside it looked all right, he thought, but knew on the inside was pain...and lots of it. A couple of times he thought about starting the car and just driving away. Maybe there was another sound that was better than George's laugh that he thought was the best, but he knew there wasn't. George's laugh was the best thing he'd ever heard and he wanted, no, needed to hear it one last time. He just thought that he would get to under better and easier circumstances.

Raine got out of the car fast before he changed his mind, and walked quickly into the building and found the front desk. When he explained to the friendly nurse behind it why he was there and gave his name, it surprised him that the nurse was expecting him. George's mother went ahead and called to let them know he was coming anyway. Raine was glad now that she did. It gave the hospital a less creepy feeling.

Raine bristled a bit as he walked down a hospital corridor, escorted by another nurse, to the recreation room where George was. It wasn't too long ago he was in a hospital for his brain tumor, and he had hoped never to step into another one ever again, that was, unless he fell unconscious at April's house and he was nearing his death. A hospital was the last place he wanted to visit. Also, this wasn't a regular hospital. This was for people with unseen scars and deeper wounds that were harder to heal.

The nurse walking with Raine was young and pretty, but there were signs of fatigue on her face and how she walked. She was professional and spoke in a friendly yet serious tone of voice. Raine couldn't help but wonder what she would be like in a more relaxed atmosphere, across a table maybe, and with a beer in her hand. That's where she belonged, he thought, considering her age.

"George has been unresponsive to his family for about eleven months now. He doesn't say much, if anything. It's difficult for him to focus. Don't be alarmed if he just stares into space. It's partly due to the meds, but mostly due to the damage of the addiction," warned the nurse.

Raine nodded as they approached the door and stopped.

"I just want to say I'm glad that you're here to see him. His mother has been the only one visiting for the last two years. Oh, and don't mind the other patients in the room. They're harmless."

Harmless? Raine thought. He hadn't even considered anyone being anything but. Before any fears could take hold, the nurse opened the door and led him inside the patient recreation room. It was large, sterile and filled with patients. Some wandered with dazed expressions, while others played cards or checkers with visiting friends and family. Raine's imagination had him expecting to see the gang from "One Flew Over The Cuckoo's Nest," but that was the extreme. This place wasn't that bad, and he was silently grateful it wasn't, though still, it was a depressing place. He was also grateful that he could easily tell who the patients were from their drab, colorless hospital gowns. He knew who to watch out for, and who was safe.

He followed the nurse halfway across the room until she stopped and pointed to a lone figure sitting and staring out a window.

"He's over there," the nurse said in loud whisper.

Raine hesitated taking the first step. He looked at the nurse, as if asking permission to approach. She nodded with encouragement.

"Thanks," Raine said, and slowly made his way over to his old friend. As he got closer, he could see that, yes, it was George, but he looked thinner, and his hair was not combed. He also needed a shave. He had patches of stubble on his face. This was uncharacteristic of George since he always kept himself very well-groomed in college.

"George?" asked Raine softly, as he stood in front of his friend.

At first, George didn't respond. He didn't even turn his head from the window to see who it was. Raine took a step closer, and even leaned toward the window to get a full look at George's face.

"George?" he asked again. "It's me...Raine Addison. From college?"

George blinked a couple of times, and then slowly turned his head and looked up at Raine. He blinked again a few more times as if trying to focus and comprehend.

"Remember me?" Raine asked.

George stared at Raine. His body made no movement, but his eyes began to register. Raine noticed and grabbed a chair. He pulled it close to George and sat down.

"We went to college together. Lived in the dorms. I went to see your mom, and she told me I'd find you here."

George squinted, taking a better look at Raine.

"Dude, what happened? How'd you get yourself into a place like this?" Raine asked, now sounding like he was back in college. He chuckled, hoping it might lighten the mood, but it didn't. Seeing he wasn't getting anywhere, he leaned closer to George and said, "Hey, I love you man. That's why I'm here." He then went to reach for George's arm to squeeze it, but stopped himself.

George saw this and looked surprised that someone wanted to touch him. He looked at Raine's face and said in a soft, gravely voice, "Raine Addison."

Raine let out a happy, relieved sigh, and then looked around the room as if hoping someone saw that he had gotten through. He looked back at George. "Yeah, buddy, it's me. It's Raine. How the fuck are ya?"

A slight smile came across George's face. "Raine Addison," he repeated.

"Dude," said Raine happily as he grabbed George's arm and squeezed it.

George flinched, and gave a wince. Raine quickly pulled his hand away. "Man, I'm sorry. I-I didn't...I was just..."

George looked away, ashamed to be in this condition in front of Raine.

"Hey," Raine whispered. "It's OK. I didn't mean to...look, I won't touch you again, OK? Look, hands up."

George looked at Raine who had his hands up as if he was in a stick-up. George nodded, as he deliberately moved his arms closer to his side.

"OK, look, I'm just going to be honest. The reason I'm here is because…well, I was thinking about my life, about things in my life, you know? Things like the best thing I'd ever seen…and the best thing I'd ever tasted. Shit like that. And then I came to the best thing I'd ever heard, and you know what? Your laugh was the best thing I'd ever heard in my entire life. Now, I know maybe for most people it would be something like, I don't know, a Beatles' song or birds chirping, but not me. Nope. The best thing my ears had ever heard was your laugh, so I thought why not find George and hear him laugh again. Crazy, right?"

George stared at Raine with no expression.

"So, I was wondering if you'd laugh…for me," said Raine. "Just once."

George continued to stare at him, expressionless.

"OK…how about…how about if we talk about things that made us laugh back at school. I mean, we were laughing all the time back then. Like, remember when we dismantled the RA's bed and put it down in the basement? He slept on that lumpy couch in the student union for like a week before he finally found it. Remember that?"

George stared at Raine.

"Or…Horny Bob? Remember Horny Bob?

Raine chuckled, but George remained still as his eyes began wandering aimlessly around the room. Raine saw that he was losing him.

"Oh my God, how about that hot history professor? You thought she had a crush on you, so you tried to seduce her…but it turned out she was a lesbian!"

George looked down at the floor, looking lifeless. Raine saw this and felt terrible that his friend was so far-gone. He looked across the room and saw that the young nurse was watching. She gave Raine a nod as if to say it his time was up. Raine nodded back, held up his hand asking for a few more minutes, and then turned back to George.

"George...listen to me," Raine began. "I don't know when I'll be coming back, but I want you to know that you were someone important in my life...you made a difference. I'm sorry we lost touch. I'm sorry I wasn't there when you needed me. I hope you can forgive me."

Raine looked down at the floor, sad. George looked at Raine. His eyes studied the top of his head, wanting desperately to connect with Raine, but no longer knew how. Raine looked back up and saw George staring at him. Raine smiled.

"I have something for you," Raine said as he reached into his jacket pocket and pulled out one of the envelopes he had from the hotel. "Take this," he said putting in George's hand. "Promise me you'll open it up and read it in thirty days. Try not to read it before then, OK? This is just between you and me, all right? If you don't know when thirty days is, maybe ask one of the nurses...if you forget. OK?"

George looked at the sealed envelope, but showed little interest. Raine looked over and saw the nurse giving him a sign that it was time. Raine nodded.

"I have to go," Raine told George. He then asked one last time in sad desperation, "Is there any way you could give me just a little laugh before I go? I'm not kidding, your laugh was the best thing I'd ever heard, man."

George looked at him. Again, his eyes read as if he

wanted to give Raine what he was asking for, but didn't know how. Raine knew it was wrong of him to keep trying, so he stood.

"OK. It's OK," Raine said, discouraged. "Don't forget...thirty days," he reminded George, pointing to the envelope. "See ya 'round, Buddy." He lightly touched George's hand, and then slowly walked away. He went over to the nurse and they both walked out into the hall.

The nurse saw how despondent Raine was. "It takes time," she told him. "Maybe if you came back, say, on a weekly basis, he'll come around. I was watching. He at least made eye contact with you."

"He said my name...twice," said Raine.

"He did?" asked the nurse, surprised.

"Yeah," said Raine, as if that was nothing.

"I'll tell that to the doctor. We've been thinking the damage was more severe, but that he remembered you proves..."

"Proves what?" asked Raine, hopeful.

"That possibly his behavior is due more to depression then brain cell damage. We'll try harder to engage him to alter his mood. If there is any way you could return on a more steady schedule..."

"I can't. I'm...I mean I don't live here. I'm only here for the day," Raine told her.

"Oh," said the nurse, crestfallen. "I understand. But thank you anyway for visiting, and for letting me know about him saying your name. It will be helpful for his recovery."

The nurse shook Raine's hand and walked him toward the main entrance. After saying goodbye, she then turned and returned to her rounds.

Raine slowly walked out the door and headed toward his car. As he did this, he thought about what the nurse had told him. That maybe George was just depressed and all he needed was some stimulation.

He saw George struggle to connect with him. It was in his eyes. Raine felt guilty leaving his friend behind, and in that condition, but there was no way he could visit on a regular basis. He was dying, and only had a short time to live. He had to think about himself. But thinking only about himself didn't mean that much to him anymore. And realizing what little time he had left on earth is what made Raine quickly turn around and head right back into the hospital.

CHAPTER SIXTEEN

RAINE ENTERED THE HOSPITAL AND looked for the nurse who took him to George. He didn't see her on the floor and felt relief since he wanted to go unnoticed as he made his way back toward the recreation room. He slowed down when he saw a utility closet, and lingered near it. When the hallway became empty, he quickly dashed inside it. The closet was a tight space, small and filled with cleaning supplies, which including buckets and brooms.

Raine eagerly searched the shelves and found in a lower corner a stack of hospital gowns, the colorless kind worn by the patients. He found one that best suited his size, and then began to undress. He removed everything he was wearing, including his briefs, put his clothes in a neat pile on a shelf, and then put on the gown. He also messed up his hair, to make it look like he had just rolled out of bed. He wanted to make sure he blended in. Raine then slowly opened the door and peeked out to make sure there was no one in the hall. As he did this, from the corner of his eye, he noticed an almost finished roll of paper towel on a shelf. He eyed it for several moments, and then grabbed it and tucked it under his gown.

Back in the hall, Raine walked slowly with his head down, as if he were a patient. He followed the same path the nurse had led him down earlier and stepped into the recreation room. No one took notice of him, not even the bulky sized orderly who was in a corner talking with a visitor, so it was easy for him to make his way back toward George.

It was in that moment that George turned his head away from the window and glanced around the room. He saw Raine and squinted with a perplexed look on his face. Raine saw him and stopped. He quickly realized he was standing next to a nurse. She was not the friendly one from earlier. This one had a stern expression and was fat.

Without her seeing, Raine lifted his finger to his lips, signaling the "shhh" sound to George, and then lowered his hand and, acting catatonic, slowly shuffled in his direction.

George watched Raine with detached interest. Raine knew his friend was watching, so he made zigzags around the room to make sure he was able to hold George's curiosity. If George was really mentally damaged, he would have lost interest and went back to staring out the window, but seeing that he was alert and following Raine's every move, Raine knew there was hope for George.

Raine finally made his way over to George and stood by him. George looked up at Raine confused, but interested.

"Hey, Buddy," Raine addressed his friend in a

whisper. "Look, I know you're still in there, that's why I came back. And you would be doing me a huge favor if you'd just laugh for me. I know it's probably asking a lot, considering your condition, but I came here to get a laugh, so how 'bout helping an old college buddy out?"

George stared at Raine as if he didn't understand what he said. Raine glanced around the room, keeping his eyes on the attendants and nurses.

"Dude, come on!" Raine whispered loudly. "It's only a matter of time before they make everyone go back to their rooms. This is seriously my last chance. I can't come back here. We'll probably never see each other again. Don't make me leave without knowing you're going to be all right. Just give me a freakin' laugh."

Raine didn't mean to sound desperate, but he was. George began to turn his head back toward the window. Raine saw this and said, "No…no! George, come on! Don't disappear on me."

The fat nurse looked over at Raine with George. A look of confusion came across her face. Raine didn't look familiar to her. Raine glanced over and saw her looking at him. "Shit," he muttered to himself, and then looked back at George.

"George, I think they're on to me. Come on, one laugh. One laugh!" Raine urged him.

George gave Raine a sad expression and looked down at the floor. Raine felt a mixture of disappointment and anger. "You're not going to give it to me, are you? Do I have to pound it out of you?" asked Raine, looking as if he was ready to strike him.

But he didn't, nor would he. Instead, he glanced

over and saw the fat nurse making her way toward him. Behind her was the bulky looking hospital orderly.

"Shit," said Raine aloud. He quickly moved away from George and shuffled over to another part of the room. The fat nurse followed him. As Raine weaved around the other patients, the fat nurse kept a steady pace with him. Not wanting to upset the other patients, or cause a commotion, she simply followed him, picking up her pace, as did Raine. The orderly began following Raine as well. Raine became more clever and quick in avoiding the two of them, but he knew he could only keep this up for so long. He kept glancing over at George to see if he was watching. He was. All Rained cared about now was holding George's interest.

"Hey, George…is this what you wanted?" shouted Raine from across the room, as he continued to outpace the fat nurse and the orderly.

Hearing his name spoken so loud, startled George, but he didn't cower. Instead, he shifted in his chair to better keep his eyes on Raine.

"Please keep your voice down," ordered the fat nurse in a loud whisper to Raine.

All of this sudden action caught the other patient's attention, as well as their visiting friends and family. Everyone in the room now watched in confusion this awkward "chase" between Raine, the fat nurse and the orderly. No one bothered to help in "catching" him as he weaved and bobbed around tables and patients, much to Raine's delight.

"Are you watching, George? All I want is a laugh. Just one laugh, man," shouted Raine.

Everyone in the room turned their attention momentarily to George, which made him uncomfortable. He looked down at the floor, embarrassed. They then looked back at Raine who was moving around the room like a frantic mouse in a maze.

"Get more help," said the fat nurse to the orderly, who quickly obeyed and left the room. "Please stop this now," the fat nurse ordered Raine.

"Not until I get my laugh," Raine shouted as he strategically made sure there were enough tables, chairs and people between them. "Come on, George…I'm running out of time here!" he said to George as he quickly passed him to avoid the grip of the fat nurse.

George watched, but didn't say word.

"I know you're in there, George. You were one of the greatest guys I knew in college. Everyone loved you in the dorm. Remember Cal? And Tony? We all used to depend on you. You were the only guy that we all depended on," Raine called out, addressing his friend, as he continued to move around the room.

"Ladies and gentlemen," shouted Raine, "That guy over there, George Doit, is one of the nicest, together guys I have ever known!"

The room, again, directed their attention at George for a moment, and then continued to follow Raine as he now raced around the room. He stopped near the back at one point, to catch his breath, but only momentarily since the fat nurse was heading fast in his direction. She stopped suddenly when the door opened and in walked another orderly and two doctors.

"Shit," Raine said again, outnumbered.

He quickly made a mad dash around the tables, rushing past the orderlies and doctors who tried hard to catch him. This really turned into a cat and mouse chase when Raine, no longer caring who got in the way, began knocking over tables and chairs to slow down his captors. The fat nurse, aghast, quickly hurried the patients and guests out of their seats and to one side of the room. It was pandemonium as Raine continued to race around just inches of avoiding the reaches of the doctors and orderlies.

This continued for another couple of minutes until Raine began to climb up on one of the tables, thinking he might table jump away from them. But as he climbed up, a doctor grabbed his gown; to which Raine wiggled out of, and now stood on top of the table completely naked except for the paper towel roll dangling between his legs.

The room gasped, and then went silent. Raine quickly went to cover himself, but realized what's the use? It was covered.

Suddenly, from the corner of the room, came the most rowdy and animated laugh. It was George. He was leaning sideways in his chair with his head tilted back, letting out that enthusiastic and vigorous laugh of his. It filled the room, and caused others to laugh along as well. Yes, his laugh was that contagious. Raine quickly turned and looked at his friend. A warm, winning smile came across his face. It no longer mattered that he was standing on a table naked with a room full of people staring up at him. His friend was laughing and it was music to his ears.

Raine, too, began to laugh. He had broken through and got what he wanted, although he discovered what he truly wanted was to know that his friend was OK. Tears of joy streaked down Raine's face, even as the orderlies and doctors helped him down from the table, covered him and put him in restraints.

As they led him out of the room, Raine shouted to George, "You rock, George Doit! Thank you! Don't forget…thirty days. Thirty days!"

George was still laughing as he looked down at the envelope that was still in his hand.

The doctors put Raine in a room and gave him a shot that contained a sedative, much against his protests and attempts at trying to explain who he was. He kept trying to explain why he did what he did even after his speech began to slur, until he stopped completely and fell into a deep, tranquil sleep.

CHAPTER SEVENTEEN

WHILE RAINE WAS UNCONSCIOUS, THE nurse who was with him during his first visit with George vouched his story to the hospital superiors. One of the janitors found Raine's clothing in the utilities closet and this confirmed the nurse's statements. They held him overnight for observation, nonetheless, to ensure his safety. It was a much-needed rest for Raine, although it was drug induced.

The following day, once the grogginess of the sedative wore off, Raine showered and dress, and then was taken into one of the administrative doctor's office for a review.

"So, you're not a patient here," said the administrator, a humorless man in his early sixties.

Raine shook his head no, too tired and embarrassed to speak. Also, his head was pounding, but he did not want to share his problem with anyone.

The administrator looked at him suspiciously. "Given your performance yesterday, you should be."

Raine sat quietly, hoping the pounding would subside.

"The nurse told me you did it to get your friend to laugh," the administrator eyed Raine carefully.

Raine nodded yes, although doing that was painful, like little knives being dug into the back of his skull. The brain tumor was growing and Raine could feel it. It was hell. The administrator sat back and stared at Raine.

"I should have you arrested," he said, "But I won't because your antics brought on a change in George Doit. He hadn't been active at all until you came along, and last night he was able to carry on a brief conversation with his doctor."

Raine looked up, happy to hear this.

"It was just a few sentences, mind you, but he spoke nonetheless. His doctors are encouraged."

Raine could take the pain no longer and achingly raised his hand to his forehead and gently rubbed it as he closed his eyes.

"Are you all right?" asked the administrator.

"It's just…a headache. I'll be all right," Raine replied weakly.

"If you'd like, I can have one of the doctor's examine you before you go," offered the administrator.

"You're letting me go?" Raine asked.

"I have no other reason to keep you here. Although you won't be leaving by yourself," said the administrator as he pressed a button on his intercom and spoke into it. "Send in Mr. Addison's friends."

Friends? What friends? Raine wondered. As he turned around in his seat, the door opened and in walked

Guy with a police officer. Raine was surprised to see them. Guy gave Raine a disapproving look as the administrator stood.

"Gentlemen, you may take your friend," he said. He then looked at Raine as Raine slowly stood. "Are you sure you don't want to see a doctor for that headache?" he asked.

Guy shot Raine a concerned look. Raine noticed and brushed off his pain with a wave of his hand. "No, I'm fine. It's going away now."

As Raine began to leave the room with Guy and the police officer, the administrator said, "Mr. Addison...next time, don't go to such extremes with Mr. Doit. We'll be watching."

Raine managed a smile, and gave a small wave to the administrator and left the room followed by the police officer. Guy stayed behind and thanked the administrator for his time and understanding.

"Thank you for explaining Mr. Addison's condition," said the administrator. "We hope...well, we hope the best for him."

Guy nodded and left the room. He caught up with Raine and the police officer as they were making their way down a long hall. All three men walked in silence. Raine didn't speak because of his headache, the other two deciding to wait until they got outside to say anything.

As they turned a corner that led to the front entrance they passed a large window. When Raine glanced out, something caught his eye. He stopped to look.

The window overlooked a garden where patients sat relaxing. Some were reading, others conversing in conversation. Nearer to the window was George sitting in a chair. The nurse who first took Raine in to see him was sitting across from him. The two were in conversation, although Raine could see George struggling to keep up with the nurse. Guy and the police officer stopped after realizing Raine wasn't with them.

"Raine?" asked Guy.

Raine held up his hand to signal that he wait a moment. He then looked out the window again and gently tapped on the glass hoping to get George's attention. The nurse looked up and saw Raine. She gently tapped on George's hand to turn around. He did. When he saw Raine, he gave a weak smile. Raine waved. Feelings of accomplishment and happiness swept over Raine as never before. This was way better than any billion-dollar business deal, he thought.

What he had done for George gave him a sense of permanence, and seeing his smile, even a weak one, was almost better than hearing his laugh…almost. That was something Raine was most sure that no money in the world could ever buy.

Raine stepped away from the window and followed Guy and the police officer out of the hospital. It wasn't until they all stepped off the curb and into the parking lot that he began to worry that possibly he was under arrest. Why else would a police officer be with Guy?

"Where are we going?" asked Raine, with trepidation.

"Home," answered Guy, stern. "April is worried sick."

Raine stopped. "Then why is he here?" he asked

pointing to the police officer.

"This is Jerry," answered Guy. "He's a buddy of mine. I asked him to come with me in case there was a problem getting you out."

Jerry stepped forward and shook Raine's hand. "Glad to meet ya," he said in a thick New York accent.

Guy asked Raine where his car was. Jerry agreed to drive it back for him Guy explained to Raine.

"Wait...I'm not going back," Raine said. "I still have a few more things to do."

Guy became impatient and irate. "Are you're kidding me? After all that happened in there? No way," he said with authority.

"Hey, you don't tell me what to do," barked Raine, offended.

"Your sister is beside herself with worry, Raine. Why are you making this so hard on her?" Guy asked, more to make a point then to get an answer.

"I just got some things to do. She'll be all right," said Raine, dismissively.

His attitude enraged Guy, causing him to take a threatening step forward. "You little shit. You have no regard for how anyone else feels."

"Whoa, whoa," said Jerry, stepping in between them. He put his hand on Guy's chest, and then gave him a nod to step away with him. Guy hesitated, angry that his chance to take a slug at Raine was interrupted, and followed Jerry several feet away before they stopped. Jerry turned and said softly so Raine wouldn't hear.

"He's dying, Guy, come on," said Jerry.

"I don't give a fuck what..." Guy began angrily.

"Hey," said Jerry, putting up his hand again. "Listen to me. I think you should let him go. I had a cousin who had the same thing. A tumor. It was horrible, and we all watched him waste away alone in a room. And it was more from being depressed knowing he was gonna die then that thing that was in his brain. Trust me, April doesn't want to see that. You be there for April. Raine still has some life left in him. Let him have it."

"But what if he ends up in more trouble, or arrested?" argued Guy.

"Yeah, so?" replied Jerry.

Guy stood there for a moment, thinking. He knew Jerry was right. Not that he agreed with it, but he knew he was right. He also knew eventually, and soon, April would have to see her brother "waste away." She was already upset and crying a lot. Maybe the less time she spent around Raine, the better. Guy nodded his head to Jerry, reached into his pocket, took out Raine's car keys and walked back over to him.

"Here," he said to Raine as he tossed the keys at him.

Raine caught them.

"Your wallet and money is in your glove compartment," Guy told him. "I'll figure something out to tell April."

"It was nice meeting you," Jerry said to Raine as he shook his hand again.

"Same," Raine said back. Raine then turned to Guy. "About my sister…" he began. Guy gave him a disinterested stare. "She lives too much in the past. You can tell by just looking at that house. Give her a future. A good one."

What Raine said was a surprise to Guy. It was the first time he heard Raine say anything that showed he had any concern for April. He was also right about her living in the past, but he didn't want to give Raine any satisfaction of telling him so.

"Come on," Guy said to Jerry as he began walking to his car. He then turned and called out to Raine, "Hey – just don't do anything stupid! I can't be dropping everything to keep saving your ass. I got a life, too, you know."

Raine waved to let him know he understood.

"And stay in touch with April!" Guy shouted.

"I will," Raine shouted back. "I will," he repeated softly to himself as he walked slowly toward his car. The headache hurt like crazy, but he wasn't going to show any sign of distress to Guy. He watched Guy and Jerry get in their car and drive away. Once he was by himself again, he was able to wince and contort his face to match the pain as he got into his car. Once inside, he sat very still and waited for the aching to subside.

CHAPTER EIGHTEEN

IT WAS TWO HOURS BEFORE the head pain passed and Raine was on the road again, this time heading for Baltimore. It was a three-hour or so trek, although this one took longer with the traffic and the many stops he had to make when the headaches became more frequent and unbearable. He had to pull over at least a dozen times when his eyesight became blurry. Out of habit, he chalked it up to being tired, until he remembered that he had a brain tumor. That reality would startle him since most of the time he felt just fine. His body was good at fooling him, and he didn't like it.

Each time he had to pull over, he would try to find a nice park or someplace scenic instead of just sitting on the side of the road. Watching traffic whiz by on a nondescript freeway was not how he wanted to waste any second of the short time he had left. He was always conscience of that, making sure every moment counted in one way or another.

He enjoyed it best when he was near water. A river

or pond, though he most enjoyed the ocean. He would park his car and pop one of the pills his doctor prescribed him, sometimes breaking it in half since he didn't like being drowsy. Just enough to get the headache to subside, and then he would recline in his car seat and count the ripples in a lake, or how many waves spread out on the beach.

Occasionally, he would think about his "former" life. He thought about his office, and those in it. He knew he would have to let them know at some point what was really going on, but he felt no rush to. He was tired of rushing, and the longer he stayed away, the more he wondered why he spent nearly all of his time, before his diagnosis, being that way.

There were times when he would watch a bird, or a squirrel and create some ridiculous story in his head about the bird or squirrel's movements. That bird is out looking for food, he thought, so he can bring it back home to his wife and children. He made up the same story for the squirrel. Raine would catch himself thinking this and laugh since all of his little scenarios were based in the context of societal norms.

Why couldn't it be the bird was simply flying because it could? And why else would a squirrel be climbing up trees except because that's just what it does? Why were there so many constant examples of how free life could be, but man chooses to ignore it, sometimes even set out to destroy it, to create something much more difficult for himself? None of it made sense.

How confusing we must look to those creatures we share the earth with, Raine thought. He would then laugh at the way he was thinking. If anyone who knew him could climb into his head and read his thoughts, they would surely think he'd gone mad. But he wasn't mad. He was right, and knew he was, as he watched yet another bird circle in the sky, and then fly away.

•••••

It was early evening by the time Raine reached Baltimore. The drive exhausted him more than it should have, so instead of going directly to his next destination, he decided to check into a hotel and rest. A couple of hours of sleep would be just perfect, and then he would go to his next destination.

He made sure to get a hotel near one of his favorite restaurants, that way, once he did wake up, he could easily walk the few blocks to get there. Before he unpacked and crawled on the bed he made sure to phone April.

Keeping his promise, he wanted to prove that he wasn't the asshole Guy believed that he was. He wasn't sure why he suddenly cared what Guy thought of him, or what anyone thought of him, for that matter, since he never cared before, but now it was vital. Having integrity was something new to Raine, and he found that he liked it. Not only that, to his surprise, it really didn't take that much work.

When he called, Guy answered the phone. Raine was glad about this since it showed he kept his word, but, more importantly, to know that April wasn't alone. She had someone, and that was a great relief to Raine.

When April came to the phone, she riddled him with questions, one after the other, and sometimes asking a new one before he could answer the last, and then she burst into tears. Raine held the phone away from his ear and rolled his eyes at this. She's so emotional, he thought, but then he put the phone back to his ear, calmed her and explained why he did what he did back at that hospital.

Once April heard the story, especially the part about the paper towel roll, she laughed. It was good to hear his sister laugh, Raine thought. He made a mental note to make her laugh more often, especially when he got back home and things would begin to get worse.

The only time Raine ditched his integrity was when he lied and told April he was fine. He didn't mention the headaches, or the numbness he felt from time to time in his fingers and hands. She didn't need to know any of this. There would be enough time to worry about those things later. For now, especially with him being away, he had to give off the impression that he was perfectly OK.

"You're not just telling me that so I won't worry, are you?" April asked.

Raine laughed and promised her he wasn't lying. He also promised her he would return soon. He had accomplished two of his tasks, and had only three more to go. April told him again she thought he was crazy, and he agreed, but he wanted this more than anything. Their conversation was playful and included each taking slight jabs at one another, which brought on more laughter. When it was over, and April was about to hang up, Raine stopped her. He spoke sincerely when he told her that he cared very much for her and wanted her happy. April was stunned. She had never heard him speak this before way. Instead of appreciating his kindness, she became suspicious, which led to Raine having to assure her several more times that, yes, he was "OK."

After the call, Raine sprawled out on top of the bed and drifted off to sleep. It was a restful sleep, and one he thought would be just a quick nap, but in actuality, turned into several hours. By the time he awoke, he sat up, surprised once again that his room was dark. He leapt out of bed and checked the time. It was midnight.

"Shit," Raine shouted several times as he hurried around the room, grabbing and opening his overnight bag, pulling out a fresh shirt and toothbrush, and racing into the bathroom. It took him all of twelve minutes to wash up, make himself somewhat presentable, and shoot out the door.

CHAPTER NINETEEN

RAINE THOUGHT ABOUT TAKING his car, but that would cost him time getting it out of the garage, so he sprinted the several blocks through the urban neighborhood to reach his destination. The jog felt good at first, but after the third block he had to slow down and pace himself. He felt tightness in his chest, and that worried him. The doctor said nothing about him having a bad heart, so he wasn't concerned about that, but still, he wanted to make sure he'd get to where he was going alive.

The streets were still familiar to him, even though it had been years since he'd been to Baltimore. He spent a summer there with several of his buddies during his last year of college. Raine had gotten a job working for a financial firm. It was mostly mailroom grunt work, but he liked the experience, as well as the knowledge he gained by being there. He would watch and listen to the big money men during their coffee breaks talk about their deals, how much they made, as well as whom they screwed over to get it. They fascinated Raine, and he wanted badly to become one of them.

When he thought about this, as he paced himself carefully though the now quiet city streets, he felt great shame. All that time learning how to become an asshole, he thought. All that wasted time.

Finally turning a corner and passing many now closed shops and stores, he came upon a quaint French bistro. To Raine's great dismay, the bistro was closed for the night, although inside the lights were still on. They were dim, but maybe that indicated that someone might still be in there.

Raine banged on the window of the front door. At first there was no response. He leaned to his right, and then to his left looking inside for any sign of a waiter or bar staff. He banged once again on the glass. Realizing his efforts were futile, and feeling disappointed, he was ready to turn around and walk the several blocks back to his hotel when suddenly he saw a young, tired looking waiter enter the main room, with his vest open and tie dangling from his collar, and begin setting the chairs on the tables.

Raine quickly banged on the glass again. The young waiter saw Raine and shouted, "We're closed" as he continued to stack the chairs.

Raine banged on the glass again anyway. The waiter placed a chair on a table, came closer to the door and shouted louder, "We're closed!" He then gave Raine a bothered look and went back to stacking the chairs.

Raine was not going to take "no" for an answer, so he continued to bang on the glass until the waiter opened the door. But the waiter ignored him, walked toward the back and disappeared behind two swinging doors that led to the kitchen.

"Damn it!" Raine muttered.

As he was about to bang on the glass once again, from those swinging kitchen doors out stepped a large man in his sixties with an apron flung over his shoulder. He peered intently at Raine. Behind him was the young waiter.

Raine's mood shifted instantly from disappointment to elation as both men approached the door. The large man unlocked it and opened it wide enough so he could see who was there, but also to strongly show that the restaurant was closed.

"What's wrong? We're closed," he said in a clipped and bothered French accent.

"I get that," said Raine. "But I was wondering if you would do me a huge favor."

The large man stared at Raine, waiting to hear what the "favor" was. The young waiter behind him was leaning his head sideways to get a better look at Raine.

"I came here one morning back in 2002, I think, and you made the best eggs Benedict I'd ever tasted. I know it's asking a lot, but would you make it for me now?"

The large man gave Raine a dead stare and asked, "Are you fucking kidding me?"

The way the large man said the word, "fucking" in his French accent, made Raine smile. It sounded like, "fooking."

"I'm not. I know it's a crazy request, but I really mean it when I say your eggs Benedict are the best."

The large man peered over Raine's shoulder, thinking this might be some sort of joke, or worst, a prelude to a robbery. "No," he said angrily. "Get out of here."

He quickly closed the door and began locking it

when Raine, thinking fast, shouted, "I'll give you a thousand dollars!"

The large man stopped. He looked at Raine, unsure, and then at the young waiter behind him. The young waiter shrugged. The large man shouted from his side of the glass, "Let me see it."

Raine was relieved that he had the large man's attention, and quickly dug into his pocket and pulled out a wad of hundred-dollar bills. He counted them fast, made a fan out of them, and then held them up so the large man could see.

The large man looked impressed. He turned to the young waiter and said something to him in muffled words that Raine couldn't make out. He then looked back at Raine.

"A thousand dollars just for eggs Benedict?" the large man asked.

"That's right. Again, I know it's crazy, but I just really, really want to taste them again. Please?" asked Raine with wide, hopeful eyes. "I drove here all the way from New Jersey."

A slight grin came across the large man's face as he shook his head and, as if against his better judgment, unlocked the door and allowed Raine to enter.

"This is the craziest thing I ever heard of," said the large man, after Raine thanked him.

"Here," said Raine, handing him the cash.

"A thousand bucks for some lousy eggs," muttered the large man, still baffled by it.

"Correction. The best lousy eggs I've ever had in my life," Raine said, smiling.

The large man stood there and counted out the cash in his hands. As he did this he said, "I'm Claude…that's Jimmy." He motioned his head at the young waiter. "I'm giving Jimmy three hundred to prepare a table for you. For me, I will make your dish for seven hundred. Give me a few minutes."

Raine nodded. He liked how Claude pronounced the young waiter's name as "Shimeeee," with his French accent, and watched him disappear into the kitchen.

Jimmy took two chairs off a small table and set them properly. He went behind the bar, grabbed a clean linen tablecloth, came back and placed it elegantly over the table. Jimmy then grabbed one of the chairs he had just set down and pulled it out. He waved his hand in a suave, professional manner, motioning for Raine to sit.

Raine smiled. Before he sat down he said, "You're good. Keep it up and there'll be a big tip in it for you."

Jimmy grinned, and quickly went back to the bar and brought out some silverware and a napkin, along with a nice, small candle. He pulled a lighter from his vest pocket and lit it. Raine gave him a nod to let him know he was very impressed.

"Can you talk, Shimeeee?" asked Raine, imitating Claude.

"Do you want me to?" asked Jimmy, also in a French accent.

"Yeah," answered Raine. "But first get some coffee, and then have seat."

Jimmy looked at Raine, surprised by the offer, and then went into action. He went behind the bar and busied himself with making coffee. Raine was very pleased with himself. He liked how money always opened doors and gave him what he wanted, and yet he felt a slight sense of guilt keeping these men away from their homes and family. Even if they didn't have families, he didn't like "buying" their time. He would give them more money before he left, he told himself. After all, money was worthless to him from here on out. It couldn't buy him the one thing he wanted most, and that was better health.

Jimmy made the coffee and served it in a cup that looked like a small bowl, and then took a seat across from Raine. He watched as Raine brought the cup/bowl to his lips, took a sip, and then placed it back down.

"That's good coffee."

"Merci," said Jimmy followed by a slight bow of his head.

Raine gave Jimmy a suspicious look. "Are you really French, or is that just an act to go with the décor?"

Jimmy grinned, and spoke in a thick French accent. "It's is quite real, Monsieur. I am from Arles, southern France."

Raine thought for a moment. "Arles. Isn't that where Van Gogh and Gauguin hung out?"

Jimmy nodded, impressed. "Oui. You enjoy art, Monsieur?"

"Not really. My sister does. A lot. I guess I was listening that day when she was talking about those two."

Jimmy laughed. "And what is it you do?" he asked.

Raine looked at Jimmy, startled by the question. Not too long ago he would have answered him instantly, impressing him about his successful deals on Wall Street. Also, it was not so long ago, he would never have found himself sitting across a table with a waiter, of all people, in the middle of the night talking about dead painters. He was strangely stumped now on how to answer Jimmy's question.

"I, uh…" Raine stumbled. "I used to work in finance. In New York," he answered. It sounded so pointless and disgustingly a waste of valuable time.

"Ah," said Jimmy, "Which is why you have so much money to buy eggs at this hour."

Raine nodded, suddenly embarrassed by this. He quickly changed the subject. "What are you doing in Baltimore? I mean, who leaves the south of France for this place?"

"The American dream," Jimmy answered.

"Some dream," Raine replied, and rolled his eyes.

"It shouldn't matter where you are, as long as you are happy, no?" asked Jimmy.

"Are you happy?" Raine asked, eager to know.

"Oui. I am very happy."

"How?" Raine asked, confused.

"I just made three hundred dollars for making you a cup of coffee," Jimmy said with a smile.

"Money isn't everything," Raine muttered as he took another sip from his cup.

"True," said Jimmy. "But tonight, because of you, I now have enough money to finally buy the ring for my love. I can propose."

Jimmy then reached in his shirt pocket and pulled out a small photo of his girlfriend. He handed it to Raine. Raine looked at it. She was an average looking girl, but her smile, and Jimmy's obvious love for her, made her beautiful.

"That's great," Raine said as he handed the photo back to Jimmy.

"We came to the U.S. together. I would go nowhere without her," he said staring at the photo.

"What does she do?" asked Raine.

"She is at home with our baby daughter."

Raine looked at Jimmy surprised. "You have a kid and you're spending your money on a ring?"

"It's what Annabelle wants," said Jimmy. "She's always wanted a ring and be married."

"Yeah, but…" Raine began, and then stopped.

Jimmy looked at him waiting for him to finish what he was about to say.

"You're a waiter and…I don't know, that three hundred bucks could go for supplies for the kid or something. Go down to city hall and just get married there."

"Americans," said Jimmy, and laughed. "I'd much rather give my daughter a show of my love for her mother then what you call 'supplies'."

"Yeah, but…" Raine began.

"Do not worry. My daughter does not starve. She is well taken care of. She does, however, need to learn about love and generosity. Those are the essentials."

At that moment, Claude came out of the kitchen with a beautiful plate. On it was exactly what Raine had ordered…eggs Benedict with a side of potatoes, roasted with savory thyme and basil.

Claude placed it down in front of Raine, and watched Raine lean over it, take in its delicious fragrance and close his eyes in revelry. Claude glanced at Jimmy. Jimmy looked at Claude. They both shrugged and turned their attention back at Raine.

Raine opened his eyes and smiled. "It smells amazing. Just as I remembered." He then took the knife and fork in his hands. Before he cut into the sumptuous meal, he stopped and asked Claude to have a seat.

Claude at first declined, but Raine insisted. Claude went over to the bar, poured himself a cup of coffee, and then came back and pulled up a chair. As he sat down, he asked, "When were you last here again?"

"Around 2002," answered Raine.

Claude smiled. "Then I was the one who made this for you the first time. I am the owner and the chef."

Raine grinned, and then cut into the French styled poached egg, slow-smoked ham and brioche. He dipped what was on his fork into the specially made Hollandaise sauce, and put it in his mouth. His taste buds came to life as he chewed. He closed his eyes once again and let out a soft "Hmmm" sound, with complete appetizing delight. Claude and Jimmy smiled when Raine opened his eyes and gave them the "thumb's up."

Raine mumbled "delicious" before he swallowed, and began cutting another part for himself.

"As good as 2002?" asked Claude.

"Just as good, yeah," said Raine as he shoved another forkful into his mouth.

Claude took a sip from his cup, and then said, "I'm sure you've eaten better things than this. This cannot be your favorite."

"It is," said Raine after swallowing. "You know,

when you think back on the best things in your life, you'd be surprised how it's the smaller things that stand out the most."

Both Claude and Jimmy nodded in agreement.

"If I had to choose my favorite meal, it would have to be…" Claude began as he looked up at the ceiling, thinking. "Lobster lasagna. I had it in London back when I was visiting once with my first wife. The best." He kissed his fingers and opened them fast toward the ceiling to highlight his pleasure.

Jimmy responded, too. "Mine is a Greek pizza with feta cheese and spinach made in this little café in New York City. I never had another one like it since. Unforgettable."

"Right?" asked Raine. "See, it's not just the actual food itself, but where and how it was made. You just never forget it. This is mine. The best thing I've ever tasted," he said, pointing eagerly at the eggs Benedict with great appreciation.

"Then I am very flattered to be your best," said Claude, bowing his head in thanks.

As Raine ate his meal, Claude and Jimmy regaled Raine with stories about growing up in France, how their paths crossed and how they ended up in Baltimore. All three men talked about music, wine and women, especially about women. Raine told them about the many beautiful women he had been with, but added how he wasn't good enough for any of them. An honest admission that he was surprised he openly shared.

"Are you married?" Jimmy asked Raine.

Raine stopped chewing for a moment. The question

strangely rattled him. Not because he wasn't, but because he knew that he would never get the chance. He shook his head and took a sip from his coffee.

"You live alone?" Jimmy inquired.

"No, with my sister. In Connecticut," Raine answered.

"But you said you came from New Jersey," Claude said, confused.

"Drove from New Jersey. I live in Connecticut," Raine replied.

"Such a long drive in the middle of the night for just a craving," Claude commented.

"It's a long story," Raine said with a smile, although he was starting to feel uncomfortable with the questions, which made him go back to his food and eat a little faster.

Claude and Jimmy noticed and, not wanting to bother him, gave each other knowing glances, stood and told Raine they were going to clean up and get ready to close, but asked him to please take his time and enjoy his meal. Raine felt bad that they felt like they had to excuse themselves, and suddenly felt alone. He finished his food, leaving nothing on his plate, and then collected everything on the table and brought it into the kitchen.

Claude and Jimmy were standing near an open back door smoking when they saw Raine enter and place the silverware and his plate on a counter. They quickly stubbed out their cigarettes, closed the door and told Raine he didn't have to bring the dishes in, but Raine told them he wanted to.

"I have something for you," Raine said reaching

into his pocket. He pulled out more cash. "Here's another five hundred for you," he said holding the money out to Jimmy.

"No, no," I cannot," Jimmy said taking a step back.

Claude stepped forward, reached into his pocket and removed the cash Raine gave him earlier. "We want to give you your money back."

"What? Why?" Raine asked.

"You've become a friend. We can't accept it now. It was only eggs Benedict. This is too much," explained Claude.

Jimmy dug into his pocket, removed his three hundred dollars and held it out to Raine.

"No. Nope, I won't take it," said Raine stepping back himself.

"Please," said Claude wanting to hand it to him.

"No," insisted Raine, holding up his hands. "Please, take this," he said holding out the five hundred to Jimmy. But Jimmy refused.

The three men all stood there holding out money that none would take from each other. It was an odd and awkward moment. Finally, Raine spoke to Jimmy.

"Consider it a wedding present. My sister is getting married, too, soon, so I'm in a generous mood. Please. I insist."

Jimmy gave in, smiled and said, "Merci," as he took the cash.

Raine then turned to Claude and shook his head at the money in his hand. Claude, knowing Raine wasn't going to take it, put it back in his pocket.

"I have one more favor to ask," Raine said as he

reached into his jacket pocket and pulled out one of his envelopes. "I want you to hold on to this, but don't open it until thirty days from now." He handed it to Claude. Claude looked at it, puzzled.

"It's not more money, so don't worry," Raine told him, "It's something…well, personal. You two have been very kind, and I appreciate it. Please, open it in thirty days, but not before. Will you do that?"

Claude looked at Jimmy. Jimmy shrugged, and then nodded. Claude looked at Raine and promised him he would do just as he asked. Raine then shook both their hands and left the kitchen. Claude and Jimmy followed him and let him out the front door.

"Good luck, my friend," said Claude as Raine stepped out on the sidewalk. "And thank you again for remembering my food."

Raine felt touched that Claude called him "my friend." Those were words he had never heard anyone say to him before. Especially not from someone he barely knew.

Raine smiled, and said his goodbye. He then turned and began the long, solitary walk back to his hotel.

CHAPTER TWENTY

RAINE LIED AWAKE THAT NIGHT, after returning from the restaurant. He thought about Claude and Jimmy and how easy it was to just sit and talk like that with two strangers. He wondered why he never did it before. He thought about the people in his office, guys like Anderson and Stein. He'd known them for over six years, and yet knew very little about them. He knew they worked hard, and that Stein liked the Yankees and Anderson was from somewhere in Maine, but aside from that he knew nothing else. Why hadn't he ever had a coffee with them, or discussed politics, or movies? Something. Anything. He knew the answer, and it wasn't just because working in finance took up all his time and energy. It was because he didn't know how.

Sure, he could talk, but never about anything personal. That always felt like he was giving something away. What he learned that night in the bistro was when you give something of yourself, you get something back.

And what he got back from Claude and Jimmy was friendship. He knew that, if he wanted to, he could return to that bistro first thing in the morning and they would both be there and would welcome him with smiles and handshakes. Knowing that made him feel great, yet learning that so late in the game made him feel like shit. Oh, the wasted time, he thought as he turned his head and stared at the wall. All the Goddamned wasted time he repeated over and over in his head until exhaustion overcame him and he drifted off to sleep.

•••••

The next morning, Raine awoke with one of the worst headaches he'd ever had. It wasn't like any of the others. No, this one was flat out excruciating. It was an intense throbbing he felt on both sides of his temples. He couldn't even lift his head. He lied there with his eyes shut tight hoping the pain would subside, but it didn't. Not for an hour.

In that time he imagined the tumor was growing at a fast rate. That's what it felt like, and that it would get so big that it would no longer keep contained in his head causing it to tear open and his brains to spill over on to the pillow right before his eyes popped out of their sockets. He hated himself for having those exaggerated thoughts, but that's what it truly felt like. He couldn't help but think of the most gruesome images and fought like crazy to think of something else.

The pills he needed were in his overnight bag, but he couldn't get up to take them. He began to wish that he never took this stupid trip and was back in Connecticut so April could help him. He wished he had told Claude and Jimmy about his condition because he knew they were the kind of guys that would have asked him where he was staying so they could check in on him that morning. They would get his pills for him and help him, but he didn't and now he was stuck.

He thought about Guy being pissed off for not going back with him when they were in the parking lot of the hospital. Everyone in his life seemed right and he was nothing but wrong. He promised himself that when, or if, the pain stopped he would call April and tell her he was coming home. He already saw Louise's legs, heard George's laugh and tasted his favorite dish. That was enough. He wanted to go home.

The throbbing did eventually subside, but even after the pain was gone Rained lied there suspicious that any movement might bring it all back again. But after about ten minutes of feeling no pain at all, he slowly sat up. He turned his head slowly from one side to the other just to make sure that any movement wouldn't make it come back. Relieved and happy that it didn't, he got out of bed and, keeping that promise to himself, phoned April.

"I'm coming home," he said to her after describing to her the wonderful meal he had at the French bistro.

"Eggs Benedict? Really? Eggs Benedict?" April asked sarcastically into the phone. "I could have made you that, Raine. You didn't have to go to Baltimore!"

"But this place makes the best," he said.

"The best, of course," she said with a chuckle. "So, how are you otherwise?"

Raine told her that he was fine. That he was in no pain. He didn't want to worry her with the experience he just had. "I'm going to take a shower and make my way home now. I should be there in a few hours," he said.

"What about the other two?" April asked.

"The other two what?"

"Touch and smell. Your five senses. You have two left," April reminded him.

"Yeah, well…I'm tired. I'm OK," Raine quickly said, not wanting her to get worried. "But, you know, it's a lot of driving and…I just want to come home now."

April was suspicious. It wasn't like Raine to quit anything he'd started, but she never let on that she was, and told him she looked forward to seeing him again. She would also have dinner ready for him.

Before they hung up, Raine said, as if an after thought, "Hey, April…I love you."

April covered her mouth, not wanting him to hear her weep. He had never said those words to her before, and they took her by surprise. "I love you, too," she managed to whisper back.

Raine hung up the phone and sat there for a moment on the edge of the bed. Why had he waited so long to tell her that? In the past, he never said it, and now he suddenly felt like he couldn't say it enough. Why? He wondered. It wasn't until he really needed her and knew that she would be there, was the answer. She loved him, and for the first time he really allowed himself to feel that, and that's why the words fell from his lips so easily. It was a strange feeling being loved. He thought about all the sexy women he had slept with and thought he loved, but didn't. And those who said they loved him, but he knew only loved his money. It all seemed like such a big waste of time. More wasted time.

Raine went and took a shower, and then dressed and packed his bag. He checked out of the hotel and was happy being back in his car and heading for Connecticut. He made sure to drive past the French bistro one last time in hopes of maybe catching a glimpse at his friends again. He was pleasantly excited to see Jimmy setting small tables outside, preparing for customers, and thought of honking his horn for one last wave, but decided against it. They said their goodbyes for good already, and that felt complete to Raine.

He drove on with a feeling of goodness in his heart, but also with some regret for never bothering to thank chef Claude back in 2002 for the wonderful dish he made. They might have been good friends all these years. But the important thing was that he knew him now, and for that he was thankful.

CHAPTER TWENTY-ONE

RAINE WISHED HE HADN'T TOLD April he'd be home in a few hours. On a good day, and if he were healthier, yes, but the drive was over three hours and with the occasional weariness, along with the fact that his eyesight would blur unexpectedly, and at odd moments, he needed to pull over and wait it out. He wished the symptoms would come all at once, sparing him these jolting reminders that he was going to die. He got it already, and cursed the universe, or God or whatever, for having to keep letting him know it. He thought about calling April, but didn't want to. She said she would have dinner ready, so maybe she understood it would take him longer. He decided to go with that thought. Whether it was true or not, it helped when he needed to pull over.

During one of those delays, once he got off the I-95 N into Delaware, he pulled over in a strip mall parking lot and did some people watching until his head pain subsided. He saw two construction workers having lunch in their truck and found it disgusting how they ate with those dirty, dusty hands. He then watched a mother push a stroller while talking on her cell phone as her small, sleeping child hung sideways in his seat, nearly falling out, and shook his head at the carelessness of this neglectful woman. He wanted to call out, "Hey, your kid is just dangling there," but he felt too weak to do it. "Good luck, kid," he murmured as the stroller and kid pushed past his car.

He saw teenager come out of a convenient store slapping a pack of newly bought cigarettes into his palm. He didn't look a day over fifteen, but Raine didn't judge. He remembered being that age and smoking his first cigarette just to look cool. He was thankful that the habit didn't stick, but thought how he could have continued since he was dying now anyway. All those years he could have been "cool," he thought, which was then followed with a chuckle. What was being cool now was not having a brain tumor. That was way cooler then having a cigarette dangling from his lips.

Raine reached over and dug out the list from his overnight bag. He unfolded it and looked at what he had accomplished so far and what he was not going to complete.

"You have two left," he recalled April saying. He stared ahead thinking about this, and then looked at the paper again. One of the last two was actually in Connecticut, on the way back to April's house. Was he up for it?

He looked at his watch, then grabbed his laptop and opened it. He forgot to charge it while in the hotel, but the battery was still good for a couple more hours. All he needed was to Google something to see if making that last stop would be worth it. To his surprise, yes, the person he hoped to see was still at the place where he wanted to go. He looked at his watch again, and then checked the area he was in. If he left immediately and made good time, meaning no more blurry eyes or headaches, he could easily squeeze in one more experience from his list. Four out of five was better than three.

With new determination, Raine closed his laptop and put it on the passenger seat. He shoved the list in his jacket pocket and, although the headache was still there, it wasn't debilitating, so he started the car and pulled out of the parking lot.

Once he merged on to the I-295 that brought him on to the New Jersey Turnpike, it was easier for him to navigate his way home. He turned on his radio at this point and listened to more oldie hits of the 90's and after. They played a few "chick" songs of that era that Raine tolerated. When the song "Sunny Came Home" by Shawn Colvin came on, Raine turned up the volume and listened intently. He never did understand what that song was about and wanted to hear the words, but when it was over, he still didn't understand it.

The song that played after that was "Bitch," by Meredith Brooks. Raine quickly turned down the volume. He hated that song, although he couldn't help singing along to the verse. It was catchy; he gave it that much. When it was over, and after a couple of commercials, the song "Hey Ya!" by OutKast came on. He turned the volume way up and rolled down his windows for that one.

He thought about how the last time he had heard

these songs he was tumor free. Or was he? Who knew how long that tumor was in his brain? It could have been there even then, but he didn't know it. What he did know was that he had no knowledge of it and how good life was, at least in that regard. But was his life ever really good? The more time he spent driving and listening to those songs, the more he realized that his life really wasn't much of anything most of the time. Yes, he had money and all the success that the world would look upon his life as, but he was really empty and alone. Life sucked, he thought, and not because he had a brain tumor.

He no longer wanted to hear any of the old songs, so he turned off the radio. He wanted to listen instead to the wind and to hear the other sounds that came from the George Washington Bridge as he drove across it. When he was half way over it, an odd thought came into his head. What if he decided to end his life by driving off the bridge? He didn't think this because he was suicidal, but wondered more about who would care? April was the only one he could think of. Maybe Claude and Jimmy. That was it. He sank in his seat, depressed and turned the radio back on. A bouncy George Michael song was playing, but he didn't bother to pay much attention to it. It did nothing to change his dreary mood.

It wasn't long before he got into New York, and then on toward New Haven, Connecticut. Once in Connecticut, he wasn't far from Darien, where April's house was. But he didn't go there. Although he was feeling exhausted and had a minor headache, he really wanted to make that last stop which wasn't too far away.

After driving down several familiar streets, he

approached his former elementary school, and slowed down as he got nearer to take a good, long look at it. It had been years since he had seen it, but at that moment it felt like centuries. He drove into the teacher's parking lot, parked and stared out at his old school trying to remember what it used to feel like being less than five feet tall, and dependent on his teachers. The school looked vacant. He checked his watch and saw that it was a little after one. He knew the kids were in there, probably learning something, but he wasn't there to see any kid. He wanted to see one of his former teachers.

He looked into his rearview mirror to check his appearance. It shocked him to see an old, tired face looking back. Being so near his old elementary school screwed with his mind and made him believe he was young again, so seeing his face, this glaring reality, made him feel like ninety, not thirty-three. He looked worn out, but not ill. He was at least grateful for that. He didn't want to look like he was going to die soon to anyone. He still wanted to keep that to himself. He wasn't sure why any longer. What did it matter?

But he didn't feel like answering his own question right then. He only wanted to look his age, so he ran his fingers through his hair and gently slapped his face to give it some color. That kind of worked, he thought. It was good enough. Who was he trying to impress anyway, his younger self? He didn't exist anymore, nor did his childhood. So, with that rationalization, Raine dug into his overnight bag, pulled out one of the last two envelopes from it, tucked it into his jacket and got out of his car.

CHAPTER TWENTY-TWO

RAINE FELT LIKE A GIANT walking into his elementary school. The halls were narrow and confining. He remembered thinking it was larger the last time he was there, but to a kid everything looks larger. The doors were once enormous and the classrooms massive, but now it was as if they had all shrunken in size. Funny how growing up makes everything from the past seem so distorted.

He thought about going to the main office, as was mandatory for all visitors, but he just wanted to go straight to his old classroom. He made a familiar turn, and then down a short staircase when a young male teacher, approached and stopped him.

"Can I help you?" he asked sounding friendly yet suspicious.

Raine felt caught. He suddenly became self-conscious and did his best not to fidget. "I was…I was looking for Mrs. Shapiro's classroom.

"Mrs. Shapiro?" asked the young teacher, as if he

needed to know more information.

"Yeah. I attended this school back in…oh, man…" Raine tried to recall the years.

"The eighties?" asked the young teacher.

Raine chuckled. "More like the early nineties. Around then."

"Is Mrs. Shapiro expecting you?"

"Uh, no…it's sort of a surprise," Raine admitted.

"Did you go through the main office?" the young teacher asked again with authority yet still friendly.

"I didn't," admitted Raine.

"Well, you can't be roaming the halls like this," said the young man as he began to lead Raine toward the main office.

Raine stopped. "I-I know that…I just…well, I just wanted to talk to Mrs. Shapiro for a moment. Really, it will only take a moment."

"I understand, but there are rules," said the young teacher as he began to walk again in the direction of the main office.

Raine began to follow, but stopped. "Look, there's a reason I'm here. I don't know why I'm telling you this, but…I'm not OK."

The young teacher gave Raine a nervous look. Raine noticed.

"No, no…I'm not dangerous. I don't have a gun or anything, I promise.

The young teacher looked even more nervous at the mention of the word "gun."

Look," began Raine, "It's just that I…I have a brain tumor…I was recently diagnosed. They gave me only a few weeks to live, and I just wanted to visit my old school."

The young teacher's demeanor softened a little.

"I wanted to come back and see...I just wanted to see my favorite teacher one last time, but I don't want her to know what's going on with me, you know? I don't want anybody's pity or whatever. I doubt she will even remember me. She probably won't, but I just wanted to see her one last time."

The young teacher looked at him, unsure.

"My name is Raine Addison. You can look it up in the records. I'm thirty-three. You can do the math to figure out when I was a student here. Mrs. Shapiro must be...well, she was a lot younger the last time I was here."

The young teacher let out a chuckle and nodded his head.

"I'm from Darien. My sister April still lives here in town," Raine said.

"Wait...is your sister April Addison?" asked the young teacher.

"Yeah," answered Raine, relieved to finally be getting somewhere with this guy.

"I know April! She volunteers during the holidays when we have our Thanksgiving and Christmas pageants. She helps with the costumes and set decorations," said the young teacher reaching out to shake Raine's hand.

Raine shook his hand, but felt like an idiot for not knowing this about April. Of course she would be a volunteer, he thought.

"She's mentioned you quite often. Said you were a big financial wizard on Wall Street."

"No, I'm not a wizard...just good at my job," said

Raine, hating to talk about what he now knew was his former life.

The young teacher quickly recalled what Raine had just told him about his brain tumor and became sympathetic. "Oh, man, I really am sorry about what you're going through. If I had known you were April's…"

"No, it's OK," said Raine. "But do me a favor. Don't mention this to anyone here. April is still trying to deal with it, and she wants to keep it private. So do I."

"Oh, of course. Yes. I won't tell a soul," promised the young teacher. "Come on…I'll take you to see Mrs. Shapiro," he said as he led Raine in the opposite direction from the main office.

As Raine followed him down the hall, the young teacher asked if he should introduce Raine to Mrs. Shapiro. Raine said no. He wasn't sure if he wanted to even talk to her, he only wished to see her. The young teacher nodded his head, understanding.

"Well, the student's lunch time is over, so I think they're outside on a break. I think we'll find her outside in the back. I'll point her out to you," said the young teacher.

Rained thanked him as they went through several doors that led down yet another hall that had painted artwork by the students taped to the walls. Raine looked at them as they passed, appreciating the smell of finger paint and Elmer's glue. They then approached two doors that led to the back playground of the school.

The young teacher opened one of the doors, allowing Raine to walk out, and then stepped outside himself. There were dozens of children running around and playing on the swing sets and jungle gym. The squeals of laughter and shouting made Raine smile. It felt good to see so much youth and vitality. He noticed a few teacher aides standing idly by watching the children carefully, and then he saw an older woman sitting on a bench on the other side of the playground, helping a pretty little girl tie her shoelace.

"There she is," the young teacher said about to point to her, but Raine touched his hand, preventing him from raising it and said softly, "I see her."

Raine stood there and stared at the now grey-haired woman he once knew. The young teacher patted Raine on the back.

"I have to get back to work. I'm sure you'll take it from here. It was a pleasure meeting you, Mr. Addison."

"Yeah, thanks. Hey, what's your name?"

"Dan," said the young teacher. "Dan Coldsmith."

"Thanks, Dan."

Raine watched Dan go back inside, and then turned his attention back to Mrs. Shapiro. She was now holding the little girl's hands and both were swinging their arms and singing a song. Raine smiled. She was still the happy, loving woman he remembered. It was nice to know that although most things changed and now seemed foreign to him, something so simple as human kindness never did.

He began to walk unobtrusively around the limits of the playground, not to get in the way of the kids, and then made his way toward Mrs. Shapiro. The closer he got, the more she came into focus. She was no longer the younger woman he had known with dark brown hair and a slim figure. Her hair was now grey, and shorter. Her face had wrinkles, but they gave her a wise respectability.

Raine stared searching for that younger woman, but she was gone. After all, it had been about twenty-six years since he last saw her, but although this older version was now before him, the woman he knew would always be the one he would envision.

By the time he reached her, and stood silently a short distance behind her, she and the little girl finished their song and the little girl dashed off toward her friends. This was when Raine made his move. He took a step forward and asked softly, "Mrs. Shapiro?"

Startled, Mrs. Shapiro turned around. She looked at Raine, perplexed yet interested. "Yes?" she asked.

"Hi. You probably don't remember me," he said with a smile as he made his way around the bench and stood before her.

Mrs. Shapiro slowly stood and studied Raine carefully. She shook her head slightly and said, "No, I'm sorry."

Raine looked down at the ground and let out a disappointed chuckle. It would have been nice if she remembered him instantly given that he surely remembered her, but he understood that would have been impossible considering all the hundreds, if not thousands, of students she's taught. He looked back at her.

"I was in your class...way back in...well, it was over twenty-five years ago. My name is Raine Addison."

"Raine Addison," Mrs. Shapiro said, trying to recall. She looked away for a moment, and then looked back at Raine, eyeing him carefully. "Why, yes! Raine Addison. Of course! My, haven't you grown."

Raine looked at her surprised. "Wait, you really

remember me?"

"Yes, you were the little boy with brown floppy hair parted on the side that nearly covered your entire left eye. I was always trying to get you to push it back."

Raine stood there, touched and impressed. "Wow. That's right. How do you remember that?"

Mrs. Shapiro laughed. "With all the hundreds and hundreds of students, everyone thinks teachers don't remember any of them. But when one spends an entire year in a small classroom with the same thirty children nearly every day, believe me, we remember," she said as she sat back down.

"That's pretty amazing," Raine said as he sat down next to her.

"Well, I've developed a system all my own for remembering. What I do is put students into categories. For instance, there are the very bright ones. Those usually stand out anyway. Then there are the ones I have an instinct will go far in life. They are usually the confident ones. Then there are the shy ones…and the troubled ones…and the bullies. That's how I remember my students. At least how I try to."

"What category was I in?" asked Raine.

Mrs. Shapiro looked at Raine sincerely. "The ones I knew would remember me."

They both looked at each other and smiled. She was right about that, Raine thought.

"So, tell me, what has my former student been up to all these years?" asked Mrs. Shapiro.

"Well, I went to college…graduated…went straight to Wall Street and made a lot of money."

"That's very impressive," said Mrs. Shapiro. "What else?"

"What else?" Raine asked, as if that wasn't enough. He saw Mrs. Shapiro was serious and waiting for him to answer, but was stumped.

"Well, I…" began Raine. "I became a millionaire."

"OK," Mrs. Shapiro said. "And?"

This threw Raine. It was obvious she was hoping to hear more, but that was all Raine had, and suddenly he felt smaller than any of those kids on the playground.

"Did you marry?" she asked.

"Marry? No. I'm not married. Haven't found the right girl yet," Raine answered with a smile.

"Did you look?"

Raine shot her a staggered look. She was subtly relentless, he thought, but that was her way, and why he liked her as a kid. "I've dated a lot," he answered.

"I see," said Mrs. Shapiro as she turned her attention to the kids running races in the distance. She wasn't very impressed, and Raine knew he was losing her interest.

"You're probably wondering why I'm here," said Raine.

Mrs. Shapiro looked at him. Raine looked at her, but then down at the ground. He hated that she could make him feel like a child, but at the same time he appreciated it since feeling that way made it easier for him to speak from his heart as children usually do. So he began.

"There was this time, when I was in your class, that I was on this playground and one of the older kids began to pick on me. Tony Crowe. He was a big kid…one you'd put in your bully category. He pushed me, but I didn't want to fight him, so I began to walk away. He followed me and kept pushing me from behind, trying to make me fall. It was really pissing me off, but I knew I couldn't take him. If I tried, he would have flattened me, so I did my best to ignore him. He kept pushing and calling me names, and I knew he wasn't going to stop, so, I turned around and told him to leave me alone, but all he did was call me a name and pushed me again. I finally pushed him back, and hard. He fell. I guess he didn't expect me to do that, but it embarrassed him in front of his friends, so he quickly got up, made a fist and punched me hard, right near my eye." Raine pointed to his eye. "All I remember was falling backward, as if the ground under me was yanked away and I was out cold. The next thing I remembered was opening my good eye and seeing you kneeling next to me and telling me to stay still."

"Yes, I remember that," said Mrs. Shapiro. "By the time I got to you, your eye was swollen and turning a dark blue."

"Yeah," Raine chuckled. "And it hurt like a mother fu—" he began to say, but quickly said, "Like hell" instead. "Then you helped me to sit up and had your arm around me, and with your other hand you gently touched the side of my face, close to where I got punched." Raine let out a sigh. "I don't know, but when you touched my face, all the pain went away. Your hand was soft and…well…I never felt anything like that before. Or since."

"I do remember," Mrs. Shapiro repeated. "You didn't cry, but your body trembled something terrible. And I remember thinking, what a brave little boy, but I wish he would cry."

"Cry? Why?" Raine asked.

"Because I knew you wanted to, but you wouldn't allow yourself. I knew if you didn't it would stay with you. Possibly even harden you. That's how it begins, you know. An innocent playground scuffle one day creates a tough Wall Street tycoon the next."

"Really? You have this down to a science how kids are going to turn out?"

"No," chuckled Mrs. Shapiro. "You could have easily become something else, but what you are now is not a surprise. I remember watching how you were when your sister came for you in the nurse's office. You wouldn't let her touch you. You wouldn't let her help."

Raine thought about this. What she said was true. He remembered, and he still had problems letting April help. He then asked her, "How'd you know I wouldn't forget you?"

"Because you let me help you, and I have a strong suspicion that I may have been the last one."

Stunned by her spot-on prediction, Raine said, "Damn, you are good."

"Thirty five years at this job, one gets good at human behavior. What you see on this playground is usually what these kids will play out in life."

Raine sat there contemplating her words.

"Did all the pain really go away?" she asked.

Raine looked at her, mystified. Then, understanding that she was talking about when she touched his face all those years ago, he answered "yes," but lowered his head and added, "That pain did."

They both sat in silence for a moment. Raine looked back at her with a sad longing in his eyes. Mrs. Shapiro gave him a look of warmth and tremendous compassion. Then, without saying a word, she reached out and gently touched the side of his face, the same spot near his eye, as she had done all those years ago. Raine leaned his face into her hand, and held it there with his own. He closed his eyes as tears gently fell down his face. He knew instinctively as a child that this woman was something special, and was grateful that she hadn't changed and that he was able to feel her touch one last time.

"Thank you," he managed to whisper.

"Thank you," she softly replied. She watched Raine for a moment longer, and then asked, "Are you all right?"

Raine opened his eyes, slowly removed her hand, and lifted his head. "I am now," he said with a smile.

Suddenly, the piercing sound of a whistle was heard, and all the children raced back toward the school.

"I have to get back to class now," said Mrs. Shapiro as she stood.

Raine stood and thanked her again.

"Will you stay in touch, Raine?" she asked.

"No," Raine answered honestly as he shook his head. "I won't be around for long, but I'd like you to do something for me," he said as he removed the envelope from his jacket. "Take this and please read it thirty days from today."

Mrs. Shapiro took the envelope and looked at it, confused. "You're being mysterious now, Raine," she said in that teacher's tone and with a smile.

"Maybe I'm creating a new category for you,"

Raine said grinning.

Mrs. Shapiro laughed. "I think so. Please take good care of yourself," she told him, and then stepped closer and held her arms out.

Raine gratefully stepped into her arms and they hugged.

"Thank you again…for everything," he said. He held on for as long as he could, and then pulled away and watched his beloved teacher head across the playground and back into the school.

Raine let out a heavy sigh, glanced at the area one last time, and then walked around the building back to the parking lot. He got into his car and sat there for a long while staring at his old school. He knew it would be the last time he would ever see it, so he wanted to look at it a little while longer. He sensed the time going by. When you know it will be the last time you see or do something, you can actually feel the moments passing, he realized. It was a strange feeling that had a sad urgency about it. As if he wanted to take all he was looking at with him, but that was impossible. He let out another heavy sigh, started his car and drove off.

Raine took the familiar roads back toward April's house. He knew it would be the last time he would get to see all the familiar streets by himself. It was as if each house, and each street corner held a simple yet special memory. As he turned the corner that led to April's street, he slowed down. He suddenly didn't want to go back, although he knew that April was waiting for him. He knew if he did, he wouldn't ever leave again. Well, maybe for a trip to the grocery store, or a pity stroll through a park where he could experience that "one last time" feeling, like the kind he just had back at the elementary school. But he didn't want that.

He stopped the car and put it in reverse. Going backwards gave him a fleeting sense that it was possible to "go back," but he knew it wasn't real. He maneuvered the car back to the corner from where he had turned and parked. He took out his list and looked at it carefully. There was only one more experience left, and then his list would be complete. He knew that if he gave in now he would always regret not finishing what he set out to do. He didn't want to leave the world with any more regrets. He already had too many of those.

Raine shoved the list into his overnight bag, and then pulled out his cell phone. He called April and told her that he had gotten a late start and didn't want to drive in the dark. It would be safer for him to find another hotel room, and he would get an early start in the morning. April believed him, though she wasn't happy. She sounded worried and asked if she should send Guy to pick him up. Raine quickly said no, and then added that he didn't want to put anyone out, and promised he'd be there in the morning. April asked several times if he was all right, to which Raine insisted that he was. One more time he promised he'd be back in the morning and hung up.

Raine felt exhausted and the headaches started to come in spurts, like flashes of lightning crackling through his skull, but he didn't want that to stop him. He knew soon they would be more consistent and he would be confined to a bed for the remainder of his life, so as long as he had the strength and determination to take one last shot at his life and freedom, he was going to do it. He quickly started the car and drove off for New York City.

CHAPTER TWENTY-THREE

RAINE NOTICED HE WAS LOW on gas, but drove out-of-town before he decided to fill the tank. He didn't want to take the risk of running into anyone who may recognize him and have it get back to April. He wondered why he cared about April finding out. Why did he care about anything anymore? He was dying and wouldn't even be around in a few weeks. Maybe behaving this way kept that reality at bay. He didn't know. It was simply the way he was, and figured it was too late to change now. He may as well keep doing what he always did.

Getting on the freeway was once again liberating. Somehow driving made him feel like there was no tumor and he could live forever, as long as he was moving. The drive was a little under an hour on a good day, but this wasn't a good day. It seemed like wherever he went the traffic was thick and heavy, but he didn't mind. Again, the car was his place where death couldn't find him.

He thought carefully about the last name on the list.

This one would be the most challenging. Maybe that's why he put it at the bottom. There were no guarantees with any of these experiences, but they all seemed to turn out all right, but this one was a real shot in the dark. This one was riding on a hunch, a big one, too. Plus, he knew he had to pick up a few things if his hunch paid off before he reached his destination.

He made a stop at one of those drug store chains, and went directly to the perfume/cologne section where they kept their bottles in locked glass cases. Raine hated those cases because that meant he had to get a salesperson to open it. That was, of course, if a salesperson was around and they even had the cologne he was looking for. This place didn't, and told he could find it at Sears. Sears? Raine thought, hating the idea of going there. It wasn't his favorite place to shop.

After getting directions to the nearest Sears store, which was a good twenty minutes out of his way, he got back in his car and made the trek. By this time, the sun was beginning to set and he was hoping to get into the city before it did. He found the Sears store, and, yes, they did have the cologne he was looking for. It took him all of five minutes for him to get in, buy the bottle, and get out. He didn't recall Sears being so efficient, but then again, he hadn't been inside one in years. He outgrew that middle class kind of shopping years ago. He chuckled at the décor of the place as he drove out of the parking lot. That was one thing about Sears that hadn't changed since he was a kid.

Raine knew the route back to the city and happy when he arrived. It was getting dark now, but the lights were bright and the millions of people rushing around made it seem like it truly did never sleep. He wanted first to return to his apartment to freshen up, and put on clothes that made him feel like his old self. The doorman looked surprised to see him and said so. It had been a while since he'd last seen him. Raine told the doorman he had been out-of-town and left it at that.

When Raine stepped into his apartment, there was a stillness that caught him off guard. It gave him an eerie sense of the near future when he, too, would be still forever. Unnerved by this, he quickly made his way into to each room and turned on the lights. He wasn't ready for his tomb, not yet. He then went over to his massive stereo sound system that took up nearly half a wall, punched a few buttons and within seconds Bruce Springsteen was singing one of Raine's favorites, "All That Heaven Will Allow." It had an upbeat tempo that Raine, and his apartment, desperately needed. He made sure to turn up the volume.

Raine began to strip as he made his way into his bedroom. His bed was nicely made, thanks to his housekeeper. The last time Raine saw his bed there was a girl in it...Heather. He smiled. She would have liked that he still remembered her name. Once all his clothes were off, he kicked them into a small pile on the floor and walked into the bathroom.

Raine loved his bathroom. He spent a lot of time and money putting in marble tiles on both the floor and walls. It also piped in the music from his stereo, so he could jam to The Boss to his heart's content with no one watching. The shower was encased from floor to ceiling in glass, with six large shower heads always set at the strength and temperature that he preferred, unlike the ninety-year old house April had, with a bathtub you had to step into and pull a curtain across for privacy. What may seem quaint to April, felt prehistoric to Raine. His was a shower, he thought, as he stepped into it. He couldn't wait for April to see it, own it and maybe even enjoy it herself.

It felt good to scrub the last few days off of his body, and rub his expensive shampoo into his hair. He loved the feeling of anything that reminded him of how he felt before he knew he had a brain tumor, that "going back in time" sensation. It chased all his other feelings of panic, anger and regret far from his mind. The Springsteen song began to fade as another started. The second one, "Out In The Street," made Raine shout out a hearty, "Yeah," and scrub his body harder with his lavender-scented English soap, and dance wildly as the water sprayed at him from every direction.

Nothing lifted his spirits like a good Springsteen song. He lathered up his chest, torso, arms and legs in unison with the tempo, and whipped his hair from side to side, then up and down, as he belted out the lyrics. He felt young again, healthy and in charge. Unbeatable, even, until, unexpectedly, the shower began wobbling, and then slowly spinning. Raine stopped, but the shower didn't. Everything became hazy, even the music faded in and out. He held on to the wall as he stuck a finger in his ear to make sure it wasn't water pressure. It wasn't.

"Oh, shit…oh, shit…" he murmured to himself as he staggered to the glass door, opened it and stepped out. He nearly fell forward, but was able to grab hold of the nearby towel rack. He closed his eyes tight, and then opened them. That seemed to help for two seconds. It made the room stop spinning at least for a moment, but then it started again. He grabbed a towel and did his best to dry himself as he still held on to the towel rack.

When it felt like the room had stopped spinning, and Springsteen's voice was once again clear and loud, Raine let go of the towel rack and began to dry himself off. If he could get himself into his robe and get to his bed, he would be fine. Just that simple task was all that mattered in his life now, not the million-dollar bathroom with the six shower heads.

He turned slowly, reached for his robe and grabbed it. What a great success that was, he thought, worthy of a gold medal, but his victory ended fast when he clutched the robe to his damp, naked body and fell to the floor.

Damn it, he thought. As long as he was on his feet, he could do anything, but he was now handicapped. The room began to spin again. The Springsteen song ended and blended into another one. Raine knew this one, but couldn't place the title. Something about a screen door slamming and a girl named Mary. It was a song he had heard thousands of times, knew all the words to, but now it was fuzzy and unfamiliar. His head pounded as he lied there on the marble floor. Why didn't he buy a carpet? He wondered. A carpet, any carpet, would have been good.

When he tried to get up his hands were numb, and he couldn't feel the marble. Springsteen now sounded like he was mumbling and far away. The room flashed into blackness then came back into clear view seconds later. Why did Raine ever wish earlier that his symptoms would come all at once and it would be over? This wasn't the way he wanted to die. Especially not in his bathroom like Elvis did, and Lenny Bruce.

Raine realized the more he fought the inevitable, the worse it was. Lie there like a man, he coached himself, you can't beat fate. So, he stopped. He no longer tried to get up, or wished the room would stop spinning, or recall a word of a song he wasn't destined to ever hear again. He brought his robe closer to his body. At least he had that to hold on to, and for that he was deeply and humbly grateful. Then suddenly, everything went black.

CHAPTER TWENTY-FOUR

RAINE HAD FALLEN UNCONSCIOUS, BUT eventually came to. However, he was so exhausted that he fell asleep, still on the bathroom floor, and found himself in a weird dream state. The dreams Raine had come like short YouTube videos.

In one he was on a football field playing solo against a full team. It was himself against eleven pro players. As they began to charge him, he easily twisted and dodged them, making his way down the field holding the ball. In the stands were April and Guy, cheering. Next to them was Springsteen, who was making passes at Louise Gardner. Raine stopped and watched. The stands pulled away fast, as if they were on wheels and being dragged off into the far away distance. When Raine tried to call out, the football team descended upon him and took him down for a tackle.

Raine's eyes opened quickly. His body ached something terrible. He was able to realize he was still on the floor of his bathroom before his eyes fluttered and he fell into a deep sleep again. In his other dreams he was a boy of seven playing with matches, and then, in another, he was a boy of thirteen stroking his crotch while looking at a magazine photo of Sharon Stone. In other dreams, he was sixteen and with his father in their garage; then nineteen and angrily slamming a door on April; then twelve asking his mother for money; then twenty-three and spilling a beer on his lap in a bar; then ten and having Mrs. Shapiro touching his face; and finally thirty-three, telling April, "I'm doing it for you," as he tried to open the door he had slammed on her when he was nineteen.

That last one caused him to open his eyes again, startled. He remembered hearing once that they say you see your life flash before your eyes before you die, but he wasn't dead. He gradually heard Springsteen's voice come back until it was crystal clear. The song was titled, "For You," from Springsteen's first album. Raine was glad he was able to remember that. It meant his brain was still working. He wondered how many songs played while he was "out."

He didn't move for fear he wouldn't be able to, and just allowed his eyes to survey the floor and the room. He saw the towel nearby, the one he used to dry his body with, but couldn't recall know how long ago that was. He then noticed the copper pipes under the sink, and did, thankfully, remember when he had them ordered and put in. He took a deep sigh. It was time to get off the floor, but he wasn't sure how. He decided to take it slow, real slow.

He moved his arm first; the one that still held his robe to his body. Surprisingly, it moved with ease. His other arm did the same. He felt no pain. He wiggled his fingers to make sure he could feel them. He did. He felt his left arm with his right hand. To his great relief, his feeling was intact. Take it slow, he told himself, as he gradually sat up. No problem. That, too, was easy. What the hell was going on? He wondered. One second he was a complete invalid and now he was in perfect health. God, he hated that brain tumor.

He stood slowly and easily. The aches in his body now were only the ones that were due to the fall. Everything else was OK. The throbbing head pain was over. He put on his robe, went over to the sink and looked in the mirror. He looked OK, just as he did when he first entered the bathroom. His hair was still damp, so he figured he wasn't out for that long. As he held on to the marble sink, just to be safe, he recalled those late night commercials about that thing elderly people wore around their necks that helped when they were home alone and fell. He thought about buying one, but he was only thirty-three, damn it. Those people in the commercials were old and had white hair. Still, it would have been nice to have someone come to his rescue when he had an episode. He wondered what time it was as he walked cautiously into his bedroom, keeping his arms outstretched, with his fingers touching the walls for support.

The clock near the bed read a little after 9pm. Raine slowly walked out into his living room and turned off Springsteen. His hearing was just fine now, and he didn't need to hear anymore. He grabbed his cell phone and sat down slowly on the couch. He put his legs up, reclining. He was going to phone April and tell her where he was. If that episode should happen again, at least she'd know exactly where to find him.

He also thought it was time he went back to April's house, but was afraid to drive. Maybe she could come and pick him up, or send Guy. He liked that Guy was dependable. That was exactly what April needed, and what he needed as well.

April answered the phone in a cheerful way, but when she heard Raine's voice, the cheerfulness turned to concern.

"What are you doing?" asked Raine.

"I'm just here with Guy," she answered. "What's wrong?"

Raine felt put off by her question. Why couldn't she remain cheerful? Her tone made him feel like such a burden, and changed his mind about telling her what he had just been through.

"Nothing," he lied. "I just wanted to let you know that I'm in New York. I'm back in my apartment. I'll be home tomorrow."

"But I was expecting you. Are you OK?" she asked.

"No, I'm not OK," Raine answered, sounding put off. "I have a brain tumor, remember?"

There was silence on the other end of the phone.

"Oh, jeez. I'm sorry," said Raine, filled with regret. "That was really...I didn't mean it."

"It's all right," said April, her turn to lie.

There was an awkward moment of silence between them.

"Hey, can I ask you something?" Raine asked. "Was there a time when I...slammed a door in your face?"

"Yes. Don't you remember?" April asked.

Raine told her he didn't.

"You were back home after your first year at college, and your car wasn't working, so you wanted to borrow dad's car. But he had already promised it to me for the night, and you got pissed. I went up to your room to tell you that if you dropped me off at my friend's house I could get a ride home from someone and you could have the car, but before I could tell you that you slammed the door in my face."

"I was an asshole," Raine muttered.

"Yeah. You were," April said.

"I was mad because you didn't have your own car. You were older than me, and you didn't have a car," Raine said, as if still trying to defend his behavior.

"I know. You made it a point to constantly tell me how you disapproved of my life by doing things like slamming doors in my face…and not answering emails or texts. But I still loved you," said April. She then added, "All I ever wanted from you, Raine, was…to know that you loved me back."

Raine was silent. He didn't know what to say.

"What made you think of that?" asked April.

"I don't know. A dream I had. I wasn't sure if it really happened or not. I wish it hadn't."

April did, too, but didn't say anything. There was a moment of silence again between them.

"So, will I see you tomorrow?" April asked, not wanting to talk about bad memories anymore. "Are you really coming home?"

"Yeah," answered Raine. "Hey…and when I do…"

he began, and then paused briefly before adding, "I promise I'll be a better brother. At least, I'll try."

April was too choked up to respond. Raine knew this and hung up the phone. He tapped his cellphone gently on his forehead, thinking. He had been hard on April most of his life, but that didn't mean he didn't love her. He did. He really did. He just never showed it. He hoped now that whatever time he had left, he could finally do that, but now he felt like shit. Knowing she picked up on his sickening, passive-aggressive behavior all those years made him realize what a pathetic asshole he really was.

"Jeez," he said, shaking his head in shame as he rubbed his eyes. He tossed his cellphone on the couch next to his overnight bag and sat up. He glanced over and saw the last envelope sticking out of the bag. He reached over, pulled it out and stroked it with his fingertips, thinking.

The last one, he thought. It was his "best" sense of smell. Was it worth going out that evening to experience, or should he just quit while he was ahead? He pondered.

He looked at the clock. It was a quarter to ten. He felt exhausted from that bathroom episode, but then again, the last thing on his list was only several blocks away. That was, if the person he needed to see was there. But it was a long shot. He thought about April again. He felt he owed it to her to stay put. However, even though he was feeling weak, he didn't want to give in and not finish his list. But he also didn't want to do anything crazy that might cause harm to his worsening condition, and possibly more heartache to April. He looked at his hand, and rubbed his thumb against his other fingers. Numb again. Shit.

Screw this, he thought. After that night he would

never have any kind of freedom again, ever. Time was no longer something to waste. He had to do it. He rose from his chair, went into his bedroom and opened a closet. He pulled out one of his best suits, a dark grey one. A Zegna. If he was going to do this, he thought, he was going to do it in style. The crisp white shirt felt good on his skin as he pushed his arms through the sleeves and pulled it snug on his body, buttoning it up. The blue silk tie, which cost well over two hundred dollars, slid nicely around his neck. He fumbled several times as he tried to tie it due to the lack of feeling in his fingers, but never gave up and managed it perfectly, thanks to years of practice.

He slipped on his Zegna laced, wingtip derby shoes and checked himself out in the mirror. Nice, he thought. He felt like himself again. Even if he did have second thoughts about going out, it was well worth just getting dressed for.

Raine grabbed a comb and ran it through his hair. He stopped only when he had every hair in place and stared at himself. He'd never go bald, he thought, but wasn't happy about it since it was because he would not live long enough to ever experience that vain crisis of most men. Going bald. In that moment it seemed so pointless a concern. At least you were alive and made it to that age, Raine thought, cursing out every man who got that chance, or ever would get it.

He didn't like where his thoughts were going, or his anger, but it suddenly fueled his need to step out and complete his last task. He tossed the comb on the dresser and quickly walked out of the room. He went into the living room, grabbed his cellphone, keys, the last envelope, and walked out of his apartment for good.

CHAPTER TWENTY-FIVE

RAINE WENT DOWN TO THE parking garage and got in his father's car. His first stop would be the West Village. Hopefully the traffic wouldn't be so bad. He could buy what he needed there, and then come back uptown to where he hoped the person he wanted to see would be in his usual place. Thankfully, the traffic wasn't bad. It was typical, but not bad. He was able to park his car in a nearby lot and walk half a block to a corner deli that had, in his opinion, the best hoagie sandwiches in the world.

As he entered the small, Italian deli, the aroma of all the imported meats and freshly made hot food attacked all his senses at once. It was one of those "ah, it's great being alive" moments that he now savored.

Raine made his way to the sandwich counter where a large, hairy man with a thick moustache and wearing a stained, white apron over a stained, white t-shirt was handling a long knife and slicing it into a long bread roll. He looked up at Raine in the middle of doing this with no fear of slicing off a finger. This was something he could obviously do with his eyes closed.

"Hi. Whatchyou want?" the large man asked, blending his words together.

"Hoagie," answered Raine.

"Size?" asked the large man as he dressed the sandwich he was making without looking, keeping his eyes on Raine.

"Large," said Raine.

"Bread?"

Raine smiled. He liked that their exchange was all one-word questions with one-word answers. "Italian," Raine replied.

The large man nodded without changing his facial expression. He looked down at his nearly completed sandwich, and added some drippy sauce to it that he squirted from a dingy-looking, plastic bottle. It looked dreadful, but Raine knew it tasted out of this world. He watched as the large man wrapped the sandwich into plain wax paper, place a small piece of tape to it and slap it down on the counter.

The lucky customer before Raine grabbed it, mumbled, "thank you" and walked quickly away.

The large man, again, without paying much attention to what he was doing, grabbed a long Italian roll from a tray of many that was just recently made, grabbed his knife like a samurai and slice into it. As he did this he began to hum, and then sing softly an old, Italian love song. Something Mario Lanza probably sang, but he sounded nothing like Mario Lanza. Raine liked his singing, though. It made the sandwich more "authentic" he thought with a smile.

He watched the large man peel off layers from the chunks of imported meats that he had just sliced and slap them on the bread. Layer upon layer of different meats, getting it good and thick. The smell and sight made Raine salivate. The large man then added green bell peppers, onions and tomato, along with a few others items that Raine wasn't familiar with. He then grabbed a different dingy-looking plastic bottle and squirted its contents on the meat and veggies, making it good and soggy. It looked a mess, but, again, Raine knew it was a delicious masterpiece.

The large man lifted the hoagie with both hands and placed it on the waiting sheet of wax paper. He had to use two sheets for this baby, Raine noticed. He taped it up good, and then slapped it hard on the counter. As Raine went to reach for it, he noticed nearby a glass counter filled with wonderful looking pastries.

"Hey, are those made here?" Rained asked.

The large man glanced over at the pastries. "Yeah," he answered.

"Did you make them?" asked Raine.

"No. The guy in back did," said the large man.

"Is he back there now?"

The large man nodded.

"Can I speak with him?"

The large man gave Raine a suspicious look, and then turned and walked over to a swinging door. He opened it slightly and called out, "Gio! Someone wants to talk to you." He then walked back to his place at the counter and nodded at Raine. He really was a guy of few words, thought Raine.

As Raine reached for the hoagie, he gave a "thanks" to the large man, but the large man was already preparing his next sandwich and didn't acknowledge him. Raine smiled as he lifted the heavy hoagie and stepped over to the pastry counter. The hoagie must have weighed a couple of pounds, Raine thought. It sure felt like it, as he leaned over and looked at the delectable tarts, cakes and pies.

A few moments passed before Gio, a young man in his late twenties, wearing a baker's apron stained with flour and cake icing, came out from behind the swinging door and looked at the large man who immediately pointed at Raine. Gio, who was still on the other side of the counter, went over to where Raine was standing, and asked meekly, "Yes?"

Raine was surprised how young the baker was. He was expecting to see some old-world gentleman with a thick Italian accent. "I was looking at the pastries. Did you make these?" he asked.

"Yes," said Gio.

"All of them?" Raine asked, surprised.

"Yes," Gio answered. "Would you like to try one?"

"No, that's OK. Actually, I have a question. How'd you learn to make them?"

"Lots of practice," said Gio with a slight smile.

"Did you teach yourself?"

"Oh, no. I went to school for it," said Gio.

"What's the best school for this?"

"The best? I'd say the Culinary Institute of America. It's upstate. It's expensive though," Gio told him.

"Is that where you went?"

Gio nodded.

"Is it four years, like a regular school?"

"Yeah," said Gio.

Raine thought about it for a moment, and then changed his mind and asked to sample one of the tarts. Gio reached in and removed a pignolo from a plate. It's a type of macaroon that's popular in southern Italy. He handed it to Raine. Raine popped it in his mouth all at once.

"Hmm. That's good," he said with his mouth full.

Gio smiled. "It's a pignolo."

"Delicious," said Raine, swallowing. "Culinary Institute of America?" he asked.

"Yeah. They have a few schools in the country. There's one upstate. It's near Hyde Park."

"OK," said Raine with a smile. "Thanks."

"No problem," said Gio, and then he turned and went back behind the swinging door.

Raine made his way to the cashier and placed the hoagie on the counter. The cashier grabbed it and shoved it into a paper bag. Raine pulled a twenty from his wallet and told the cashier to keep the change as he grabbed the bag and left the deli. He wanted to get back uptown before it was too late.

He sprinted to his father's car, opened the trunk, placed the hoagie inside, and then went to the passenger side of the car and opened it. He reached into the glove compartment and took out the cologne he had purchased earlier from Sears. He unwrapped it, took the bottle out and placed it back in the glove compartment. He took the box and wrapper, tossed those inside the trunk, and then closed it. Now he was ready to go, he thought, as he got inside the car, started it and drove off.

As he made his way through traffic, Raine thought about where he was going. It was a bar on the Upper East Side where he used to hang out when he first landed the position at The Private Client Financial Group. Almost nightly, after work, he and a group of fellow career-hungry young men just like himself, gathered to drink and talk about money and how to make a lot of it. His best friend at the time was Paul Winston. They were a lot alike, and were on the fast track to being the best. That was their shared goal.

Raine recalled how Paul introduced himself first. He was a good-looking guy from New Jersey with a winning smile and a good heart that he hid well in the office. No one knew that side of Paul except Raine. When it came to business, Paul was as hard as the rest of them, but to his friends he was a sweetheart. Raine envied that about Paul. He had a lot of friends outside the company, and was able to turn off his business side completely when he was with them. One could never even guess what Paul did for a living if they met him casually at a party, and most were surprised when they learned. In short, Paul knew when being an asshole was necessary and never hesitated being one, but also knew when to turn it off. Raine, however, was just an asshole all the time.

It had been years since Raine last saw Paul. They once were close, real close, but something happened to Paul that Raine never understood. At the firm, they were competitors, but were always happy for each other when one would make a bigger and better deal. It was a healthy competition, and it made Raine feel like Paul was the brother he never had.

Then, one day, Paul got a promotion. It was the promotion that both were vying for. Raine didn't feel at all jealous when it happened. He was, in fact, glad that Paul got it and no one else. At least one of them did, was Raine's attitude, and he knew Paul felt the same. But the day after getting the promotion, Paul suddenly quit the firm. Just like that, and with no explanation. It was puzzling to everyone, especially Raine.

There was no "goodbye," or anything from his friend. When Raine tried to get in contact with him, Paul would never respond. The promotion naturally went to Raine after Paul's abrupt departure, and with that promotion Raine stopped going to the bar. He felt he was no longer one of the hungry wannabe's. He was above that now.

Months later, Raine found out that Paul went to a competitor, and because of that, Raine stopped trying to reach his friend, but he always kept tabs on him. Finding out through the industry grapevine how, and what, Paul was doing. He knew that, unlike himself, Paul returned going to the bar to hangout with other Wall Street guys. That was the difference between Paul and Raine. Paul never felt he was above anyone, or anything. Again, Raine was always the asshole.

If Raine knew one thing about his old friend, Paul, he was a creature of habit, so he knew he would be at the bar that evening. Paul loved being around people, and it was his favorite place to unwind. He would be surprised if Paul wasn't there. So, with great confidence in this belief, and the need to see his old friend one last time, he pulled his car into a parking structure up the street from the bar, paid the forty bucks it cost to keep it there for a few hours, and walked his way toward his old drinking hole.

CHAPTER TWENTY-SIX

RAINE ENTERED THE BAR AND was happy to see it crowded with customers, mostly young men who looked as he did ten years earlier. They sat in small groups, in suits with loosened ties, either talking about how to make a lot of money, or flirting with the attractive women that they hoped to score with. Nothing much had changed of the décor either. The TV over the bar still showed a sitcom rerun with the volume down that everyone ignored, and the house music was the latest top 40 piped in from a back room stereo system.

The bar staff were older men who looked upon the younger men as something they wished they were at that age, but somehow missed the chance, and the waitresses were working girls, polished enough to have the job, most likely to help them through college, but not attractive enough to catch the eye of one of the up and comers.

Raine's eyes darted about, hoping to find Paul Winston. He looked at his watch. It was a little after eleven now, still early for a New York City bar. He had trouble focusing on the faces of the customers. His eyesight was still switching from sharp to blurry, which worried him. Not so much because it was a stark reminder of his mortality, but more because he wanted to get through this last evening in one piece.

None of the customer's faces looked familiar. He suddenly realized he was looking for the Paul as he remembered him instead of how much older he would be now, so he turned his attention from the younger men to the more mature ones and eventually honed in on a small group at the end of the bar that were more his age.

He squinted as he focused on one of them who looked like Paul, except his hair was shorter, and his face more full then the lean, chiseled one he remembered. As he began making his way toward them, gingerly pushing through the crowd, Raine was able to overhear the voice of the man he was heading toward. Yes, it was Paul Winston.

Raine went around the bar crowd and stepped up behind Paul who was in the middle of telling a story about a recent deal he had made, which the other men loved hearing about. When he finished, Raine tapped him on the shoulder. Paul turned around on his stool.

"Hi, Paul," Raine said wearing a warm, friendly grin.

Paul's face froze with startled surprise, and then, as if blinded by rage, he hopped off his stool, made a fist and threw a hard punch straight into Raine's face. Raine staggered back and fell to the floor, knocking over a chair on the way down. The men around Paul were too stunned to move as they watched Paul take several steps toward

Raine and stand menacingly over him.

"You lousy son-of-a-bitch," Paul hissed through gritted teeth.

Raine heard these words, but they sounded distant and scratchy, as if Paul was saying them through a megaphone from ten miles away. Raine rolled to his side, as if trying to get up, and then to his other, but the floor felt like it was tilting when he did. When he moved his head he heard crackling sounds from inside, as if his brain was a potato chip bag being crinkled. He looked at the legs and shoes around him that were now at his eye level, but they were out of focus and looked like moving, blurred colors of dark blue, black and grey.

Someone tried to help him up by grabbing his arm, but Raine was like dead weight and couldn't be moved. Someone else squatted down next to Raine and asked in what appeared from Raine's point of view, slow motion, if he was all right. Raine tried to answer, but his lips couldn't form the words. He closed his eyes momentarily and asked God, or whoever of greater power might be listening, to help him, but it was of no use. He lingered on the floor like a wild animal shot by a tranquilizer dart.

Suddenly, he felt his body being lifted. He stood wobbly on his feet; once again, face to blurry face, with Paul Winston. Paul just stared at him, ready to punch him again, but someone held him back. Raine then felt his body being placed in a chair at a table. His head wobbling like a bobble-head. It eventually hit the table where it stayed. He turned his head sideways and kept his eyes open. He was glad that at least the room and all its occupants were beginning to come into clear focus. He knew once that happened, it meant the episode was ending.

Someone brought over some ice wrapped in a bar rag, lifted his head and placed it under his face. The coolness felt good on the now throbbing skin beneath it. Great, Raine thought, he was going to have a nasty bruise that he would have to somehow explain later to April.

Suddenly, the sounds of the bar became more audible. The clanking of glasses, the murmured concerns of customers mingling around the beaten guy at the table, and the music, something by Bruno Mars, was all Raine could make out.

The chair next to him pulled out and down sat Paul Winston. He leaned down a bit, coming face to face with Raine and asked, "You OK?"

Raine could only manage a slight nod.

"What the hell are you doing here? You got a lot of nerve after all this time," Paul said sitting back.

Raine felt it was safe to try to lift his head, which he did, slowly, holding the bar rag to his face. "Good to see you, too, again, Paul," he said in a wise cracking sort of way.

"You went down pretty hard. Either my punch has improved, or you've become a real lightweight," Paul said in a friendly manner, although he hated himself for not just walking away, which is what Raine deserved.

"I've become a lightweight," admitted Raine.

Just then, one of the older bartenders came over and put a whisky down in front of Raine. "It's on the house. For not dying on the floor," he said as he walked away shaking his head.

Raine winced, embarrassed. Paul laughed.

"So, you are you going to tell me why you hit me?" asked Raine.

Paul looked away, pissed off by the fact that Raine didn't know. He looked back at Raine and shook his head. "Typical Addison. You manage to fuck with people's lives, and then have no idea that you did."

Raine looked at him puzzled. He took hold of the whisky shot glass and gulped it. It burned as it made its way down his throat, but it was good. "Enlighten me," Raine said with cocky confidence.

"I ought to hit you again," said Paul, his anger building.

Raine tilted his head, confused. "Why? We were best friends, and then you quit and just disappeared. What happened?"

"You really don't know?" asked Paul.

Raine stared at him. It was obvious he didn't.

Paul sat forward. "The day I got that promotion, we decided to go out and celebrate…"

"Yeah, I remember," said Raine.

"You said you couldn't make it, or would try to make it later, if you could. But you never did."

"You're mad because I didn't come to your party?" asked Raine, confused.

Paul shook his head, disgusted. Raine glanced around the room, trying to recall details of that night ten years ago. Suddenly, he grinned a sly grin and said, "Oh, yeah. I was...delayed."

"Delayed?" asked Paul.

"I had a date. Man, she was hot. So well worth missing your party for."

"Was she?" asked Paul.

"She was in love with me," Raine chuckled, reclining back in his seat, still holding the bar rag to his face. Then he sat forward. "But it was an easy score, you know? I couldn't pass it up. You got the promotion and I was happy for you. Really, I was, but I was also kind of jealous. Not a lot...just a little," admitted Raine.

Paul stared at him, looking displeased.

"OK, a lot. I didn't want to come here with everyone congratulating you. I admit it. Call me a sore loser. So, instead I took off with a girl to drown my sorrows. I would have shown up later, but the chick was really into me, but then got crazy emotional on me after. She wanted me to propose, or something, but I was just looking for a good time. The sex was great until she went all psycho on me."

"Psycho?" asked Paul.

"Yeah...confused fucking with love," said Raine.

"Man, you're more pathetic than I thought," said Paul, shaking head.

"Oh, really? If I recall, you weren't much of a boy scout either back then."

"Do you even remember her name?" asked Paul.

Raine gave Paul a pitiful look. He was acting like a chick, like that Heather chick, to be exact. "Yeah," said Raine. "Connie something. She worked in accounting."

"Connie Nashlee," said Paul.

"Yeah. Whatever," Raine responded.

"My fiancé."

Raine froze. His eyes searched Paul's for any sign that he was joking. He wasn't. "Your...what?"

"My fiancé," repeated Paul. "We had been dating for about eight months, waiting for me to get that promotion so we could get married."

"Are you fucking with me?" asked Raine, feeling his heart and stomach sinking.

"No," Paul said bluntly.

"Why didn't you say something? You never told me you were serious about anyone…"

"We didn't want anyone to know. It was against office policy and we had to keep it a secret. She was going to quit after I got the promotion and we were going to get married. I spent the entire time at that party looking for my best friend and my fiancé. Some fucking party. You, I never saw that night, but after, Connie and I met up. I got down on my fucking knee with a ring, doing everything right, and she blurts out that she just had sex with you and was in love with you. My best fucking friend…my big fucking night!"

"Oh, jeez…" groaned Raine, looking away.

"And I knew, for you, she was just some "easy score," and I tried to tell her that, but she told me that you promised to marry her and that it was over between us. Did you fucking promise to marry her?"

Raine's bruise began to throb. In fact, his entire face and head was throbbing. Feeling like the biggest heel on the planet, he looked down and said ashamed, "Yeah."

"Why?"

"To…shut her up. Anything to get her to stop crying," admitted Raine.

"And you probably fucked her again. A few times, knowing you. Take whatever you can, right?"

Raine slowly nodded his head.

"So predictable, Addison. So fucking predictable," Paul said disgusted.

Raine sat there, hating himself. He then looked up and asked, "So, you quit and walked away from a promotion because of her?"

"I loved her! That's one thing you never got, Addison. Nothing mattered to you but you and your freakin' need for success. You never got there were more important things in life than that. Things like respect and honesty…and love. Real love. Not whatever you did in replace of it," shouted Paul. "Yeah, I walked away from that promotion, and the job, because I needed to keep my self-respect intact, and not turn into a cold, heartless liar like you. And the only way for me to do it was to get as far away from you as possible."

"I didn't know she was your girlfriend," Raine said in his defense.

Paul shook his head and let out a slight chuckle. "You think I'm pissed because you fucked Connie?"

Raine looked at Paul, mystified. Was there another reason? He wondered. Now he was really confused.

"I could have forgiven you for doing what you did because, right, you didn't know. And I could have even forgiven her because that's how much I loved her. We would have somehow worked it out, but there was no chance for that because you were so convincing in making her believe you'd marry her. She was in love with you, and I couldn't say a damn thing to make her believe otherwise. And believe me, I tried. I told her things about you that would have made any rational person want to stay clear away from you, but she wouldn't believe me. She kept saying, 'You're just jealous.' And yeah, I was. I was always jealous of you, Addison, but now, for the life of me, I don't know whatever for."

"What, uh…what happened to her?" Raine asked sheepishly.

"She phoned me a couple of months later and told me she made a mistake. She said she tried to see you again, but you ignored her calls and acted like you didn't know her when you saw her in the halls."

Raine wished the tumor would explode in his head at that moment and kill him instantly. He made no comment.

"She told me she left the company due to the stress of seeing you every day, and asked if there was anything left of what we had."

Raine looked at Paul, hoping for a happy ending here.

"I told her no. I moved on," he said, sitting back in his chair. "That was the last I'd heard from her. Who knows where she is now. I quit, went to another firm, was made junior partner in a year, and I'm now a partner."

"That I know," admitted Raine.

Paul looked at him, surprised.

"I followed your career. Well, not like a stalker, but, you know, I'd ask around…and read about you here and there."

"Why?" Paul asked.

"Because I cared. You were my friend," said Raine, knowing that sounded hollow and empty by that point.

Paul let out a snide chuckle. "Friend. Right," he said

as he rose from his chair. "Asshole," he whispered as he turned to leave.

"Hey, where are you going?" Raine asked.

"Home. It's late...and I feel better now that I got to belt you in the face after all these years."

"So, you're just going to walk away from me? Just like that?"

Paul looked at him and shook his head. "Give me one good reason why I should stay."

Raine held the bar rag closer to his face, as if to give him a second or two to figure out what to say. It would have been the perfect time to tell Paul about the brain tumor, and the short amount of time he had left to live, but he didn't want to. This time is wasn't because he hated pity, but because having a tumor suddenly felt like the wrong reason for Paul to stay. Raine wanted him to stay because he wanted to.

"Can I buy you a drink?" he asked.

Paul looked at him as if he were crazy. "Are you serious? You have a lot of nerve, Addison," he said as he turned again to leave.

"I'm quitting my job," Raine called out.

Paul stopped and gave Raine a suspicious look. "You're what?" he asked.

"I'm quitting...tomorrow," said Raine.

Paul gave Raine a long, hard stare. "You? The great Raine Addison is quitting? Why?"

Raine sat back and grinned. "I guess I got tired of being an asshole."

Paul let out a laugh. "Addison, you'll always be an asshole."

"Probably, but I am leaving."

"Did you get fired?" asked Paul, but then quickly said, "No, wait, you just landed that seventeen billion dollar account."

Raine gave Paul a surprised look. Paul hated himself for giving himself away.

"OK, OK…so, I've been keeping track of you, too. So, sue me," Paul said as he grabbed the back of the chair, pulled it out and sat back down, caught.

Raine grinned. He got his old friend to sit down. He chuckled, and then began to laugh. Paul laughed right along with him.

"You're such a liar, you know that?" Paul said.

"I know, but it is true. I am leaving the company."

Paul stopped laughing. "For real? But you are the company."

Raine smiled appreciating the compliment. He waved at the bartender and motioned for two whiskies. The bartender nodded. Raine looked back at Paul.

"They'll survive without me," Raine said casually.

"What are you going to do?" Paul asked.

His question threw Raine for a moment. He wasn't going to "do" anything. He didn't have that time anymore. That reality gave him a pit in his stomach, but he didn't show it. Instead, he smiled and said, "Just weighing my options and preparing myself for a new adventure."

Paul looked at him, unsure. This wasn't the Raine Addison he knew. Raine was always confident in what he was doing and where he was going. It had to be a trick he was trying to pull.

"I hope you're not thinking of coming over to my

firm. You can get that out of your mind right now," Paul told him with a sense of worry in his voice.

"Nah," Raine said taking the bar rag away from his face and placing it on the table. "I'm heading for something outside of all that."

"Outside of finance? Are you going into some Internet business?" asked Paul.

Raine laughed. "No. I'm really not sure yet, but whatever it is, I can assure you, it'll be big," teased Raine.

Paul sat back and looked at Raine, studying his face. What the hell was going on here? He wondered. Then he focused in on the bruise that had formed on Raine's face. His left cheekbone was now a swollen mass of dark purple and blue.

"Jeez, I really hit you hard," said Paul.

Raine gently touched his cheekbone and laughed. "I deserved it," he said, and then leaned forward. "Paul, really, I am sorry about Connie and all that."

Paul waved his hand, not wanting to talk about it any longer. The bartender came by with two more shots of whisky and placed them on the table.

"How 'bout a bottle?" Raine asked Paul.

Paul let out a friendly sigh. "Sure. Why the hell not?"

Raine looked at the bartender. "Do you have Bushmill...'92 or '93?"

"I think we have a '93, but it's pricey," answered the bartender.

"That's fine. Bring it over," said Raine.

The bartender nodded and walked away.

"Maybe you should save your money now that

you're out of work," said Paul with a chuckle.

Raine grinned. "You may not believe this, Winston, but I'm beginning to realize that money isn't everything."

Paul let out howling laugh. "Oh, Jesus! Either you've lost your mind, or you just found out you're dying."

Raine froze for a moment, thinking somehow his friend might know what's going on. But his laughter made it obvious he had no idea and was kidding. Raine chuckled along, and tried not to look like a truck was about to hit him. Thankfully, the bartender appeared with the bottle of Bushmill and placed it on the table just in time.

"Thanks," said Raine, as he reached in his pocket and pulled out a small wad of cash. He counted out several hundred-dollar bills and handed them to the bartender. "Keep the rest."

The bartender thanked Raine and walked away as if he just won the lottery. Raine reached for the bottle, opened it and began to pour the liquid into Paul's shot glass. He poured some into his, but not a lot. He wanted to make sure he kept his head as clear as possible that night, and then he raised his glass. Paul raised his.

"To old friendships," Raine proposed.

"To old friendships," repeated Paul, and then quickly downed the drink.

CHAPTER TWENTY-SEVEN

IT TOOK LESS THAN AN hour for the whiskey to hit Paul's system and turn him into a semi-functional mess. As for Raine, he was calculating and steady with his intake, and was able to stop after only three shots. By that time, Paul was unable to even notice or care. It was a surprise to Raine that Paul could still stand after Raine grabbed the bottle and suggested they take a walk around the block. He thought maybe the cool night air would sober his friend up a bit.

Thankfully, there was no stumbling out the door, and Raine only had to grab hold of Paul's arm twice to make sure he didn't. Once outside, Paul was walking easily by himself. He swayed a little, but nothing obvious. His mannerisms and diction were a different story. He waved his arms dramatically when making a point, and slurred half of his words, but this made him look like a frustrated, out of work actor instead of a drunk, so there weren't many odd looks from passerby's on the street.

The walk and night air did help enough for Raine to find out more about his old friend. Paul freely doled out information without any suspicion as to why Raine was asking so many questions, and became exceptionally sentimental when Raine began to reminisce about old times.

"Remember when we first started out, and we made that bet about who would be the first to make a million?" Raine asked.

Paul laughed. "Yeah. We carved the dates on the wall under the sink in the bathroom. You beat me by a month," he said as he lazily fondled his tie.

"The dates are still there. From time to time I would squat down to take a look at it," admitted Raine.

"Really? You did that?" asked Paul, touched.

"The times when I needed to be reminded of who I was," said Raine.

Paul threw his arm around Raine's shoulder. "Who you was," Paul said sloppily, "Was not a nice guy." He then gave Raine a gentle punch on his chest.

"I know that," said Raine.

"I mean, later on...later on..." said Paul, hanging on his friend. "In the beginning you were great."

Raine appreciated hearing that there was at least one time in his life when he was something better than who he became.

"Hey, remember when we used to take drives out to Long Island?" asked Raine.

Paul stopped, removed his arm from around Raine's shoulder and stared at him with his bloodshot eyes. "God, I miss those days," he said, looking as if he was ready to cry.

"I miss you, Raine Addi…something." He looked down at the sidewalk as if trying to remember Raine's last name.

"Addison," said Raine, smiling.

Paul's head snapped up immediately. "Yes!" he declared. "That's it. Addi-son. Addi-son. I'll never forget it."

They continued to walk together in silence. They walked around the block once, and then headed across the street to the parking lot and Raine's car.

"Where's your car?" asked Raine.

"I cabbed it," answered Paul.

"Are you still living on the west side?"

"Nope. I bought a brownstone in Brooklyn."

"Brooklyn?" asked Raine as if he told him Kansas.

"Hey! Brooklyn's nice…and it gets me out of this sewer every night. To save my sani…sani…sani…"

"Sanity?" asked Raine.

"Yes! Sanity. Thank you," said Paul with a bow of his head that he quickly snapped back up.

"You're welcome," chuckled Raine, as he went to the trunk of the car and tossed in the half-filled bottle of Whiskey. Paul watched with surprise.

"A Lexus? You're driving a Lexus?" he asked followed by a sharp peel of laughter.

"It was my father's car," Raine replied, surprised that he still felt embarrassed by this.

Paul quickly stopped laughing. A wave of sadness came over him. "Your dad. Wow. I'm sorry. That was a tough time," he said looking away, remembering.

Raine didn't want to go there, so he closed the trunk and went over to the passenger side of the car and unlocked it for Paul. Paul watched Raine open the door and motion for him to get in. Paul didn't move.

"Why?" Paul asked.

"Why? Because I'm taking you home," answered Raine.

Paul brushed away what Raine said with a wave of his hand. "No. No," he said, and then asked, "How come...home come you never...cried?"

"What are you talking about?" asked Raine, feeling his guard going up.

"I'm talking about your dad...and your mom," said Paul taking a step toward Raine, and then stopping. He put his hand on the car to steady himself. "I remember when it happened. We were at a bar, and you got a call on your cell. I watched you stick your finger in your ear and walk away from the noise. You then came back and asked me if I was doing anything the following weekend. I said I was free and asked where we were going, and you said, 'my parent's funeral. April just phoned. They're dead.' Just like that. No emotion. Nothing."

"I was in shock," said Raine, looking away and growing uncomfortable.

"I was, too, and burst into tears," said Paul. "Losing your parents at the same time. Jeez."

"Yeah," whispered Raine, fighting the memory.

"I mean, we all deal with death in different ways, but still. You never cried. You never even cried once at the funeral. I watched you, Addi-son, and waited for it, but you never did."

Raine managed a smile. "Sorry I disappointed you, now get in the car."

"No. No, no, no. I'm not getting in the car until I see you cry," said Paul bobbing his head in several directions instead of being able to shake it no evenly.

"You want to see me cry?" asked Raine.

"Yes," demanded Paul. He leaned on the car and made two feeble attempts to fold his arms in defiance before he succeeded.

"OK," said Raine as he closed the passenger door.

He stood there, staring down at the ground for a moment, and then looked up at Paul. "I remember that night, too. We had secured the Kennedy account, twenty three million dollars, and I got promoted. I was feeling great that night at the bar, top of the world, and then my phone rang. I was surprised I even heard it. It was April. She was hysterical, and told me mom and dad were killed. It was surreal. That's what it was…surreal. You took me outside, and we walked I don't know how many blocks. You cried, but for some reason I couldn't," said Raine softly.

"In thinking back now, I guess it was just too hard to believe that it was possible. How do you accept something like that? How do you accept that life could end so instantly? When we come into this life, Paul, it's planned. There are nine months to think about it, prepare for it, wrap your head around it, you know? But death? It creeps up on you like a fucking leopard in the jungle and lunges at you when you least expect it, giving you no fucking time to even think about what the hell is happening. Your head spins as your guts are being ripped out, and you're asking stupid, unanswerable questions like, "Why did this happen?" and "Why didn't I see this coming?" Or, "Can I turn back time for a just a few minutes and get myself ready for this at least?" But no, you don't get that luxury. You get the hard slap in the face that leaves you numb. So freaking numb that you feel like you died, too. But you didn't die. You wish you could, if only to turn off the pain, but no, you're still alive. You have to fucking deal with it."

Raine looked down at the ground and kicked a few pebbles away from his shoe. "I wondered that night, and even at the funeral, what it was going to be like when I died," Raine said. "That's what I was thinking. Would I go quickly like them? Or would it be a slow..." Raine's voice cracked which caused him to stop. He cleared his throat, and then continued. "A slow death. Would I get enough time to see the leopard in the jungle and be able to get away from it? And if I couldn't get away from it, would I at least have time to wrap my head around it, maybe plan for it? But you know what? Either way, there is no such thing as enough time.

"Life is..." Raine began, as tears well up in his eyes causing him to stop. He found himself fighting the tears, and knew it was a stupid thing to do, so he let them fall, as he continued. "Life is all we have. Time is all we have. Five years, twenty years, fifty, eighty years...whatever it is, it's never enough. We may think that it is, but really, it isn't. And life is going to keep on going with or without you. And that's a lonely fucking feeling. I thought I could outrun that leopard, but I can't. No one can fucking...outrun the..."

Raine finally broke down, weeping real tears.

Paul stood there, staring at his friend. He then

slowly walked over to him, placed his hand on his shoulder for comfort and said, "Man…I feel like I'm gonna throw up."

Raine looked up at Paul, realizing he was wasted and didn't hear a word he said. He even forgot he asked to see him cry. Raine let out short spasms of laughter as he wiped his tears away. The dumb jerk, he thought.

"I got an idea," said Raine. "Let's take a drive out to Long Island. Like old times."

Paul's bloodshot eyes lit up. His nausea passed. "Yes! Addi-son, that's the best suggestion you've made all night!"

Raine smiled and opened the passenger door again. Paul staggered over to it and crawled inside the car. Raine closed the door and went around to the driver's side. He shook his head in disbelief as he did this and muttered, "My one real moment, and the guy fucking misses it."

CHAPTER TWENTY-EIGHT

RAINE WAS GLAD TO GET out of New York City again. It had been over two years since he'd been to Long Island, and was happy taking the trip this time, his last time, with his old friend. Paul slouched in his seat, staring out ahead and grinning like a damn fool. They talked about simple things on the way, such as how clear the sky was, the difference between city living and suburban living, other friends who have fallen out of their lives...and women.

Oddly, there was never one mention of money or finances. That was the one topic that the two used to spend hours discussing. This occurred to Raine halfway through the conversation, and he chalked it up to how they finally had all they wanted and needed in that department, so there wasn't much to discuss anymore. He was also relieved that it was never brought up since money was so pointless to him now.

The trip to the island would take about an hour, to

which Raine was glad since it was already way past midnight and he wanted to complete his last "experience," his favorite sense of smell, before he returned to the city, dropped his friend off and got back to Connecticut in the morning. Traffic wasn't too bad this time of night, so he made it easily to the Brooklyn Queens Expressway, and then to the Midtown Tunnel and on to the Long Island Expressway. Having Paul with him made the time go by faster. It was nice to have someone along for the ride with him. The last few days were very lonely, a loneliness that he wasn't aware of until he had someone sitting next to him. He regretted losing touch with Paul, and mourned silently that this time with him would be short, and his last.

When Raine finally made it on the Northern State Parkway, and then onto Deer Park Road to Jericho Turnpike, he steered the conversation from simple banter to something more real and important.

"Paul, do you remember that first meeting we had? It was our first big account with Osko-Freed?"

"Hell, yeah!" shouted Paul, still wasted, but a little more focused. "We were nervous as fuck!"

Raine laughed. "I know, I thought I'd shit my pants. We both were out to clear over two hundred grand a piece."

"After taxes," Paul said, grinning.

"Yeah...after taxes. Remember what you did before we went into the meeting, when we were in the men's room?"

Paul stared straight ahead and began to giggle. He didn't answer, and Raine didn't push for one. Just hearing his friend's giggle made it clear that Paul did remember. Raine smiled as he watched the road.

It was dark, and a bit hard to see, but he drove straight on through into a small town called Northport that was on the Northern Shore of Long Island, and followed the familiar streets that led toward a long stretch of road called Eatons Neck. Both he and Raine discovered this area many years ago during a Fourth of July picnic thrown by one of the partners of their company. A rich bastard, Raine remembered, who always gave the newer guys a hard time, cracking the whip and never letting up with his insults and sense of superiority.

It was a complete surprise when the rich bastard invited everyone in the company to his home out on the island, which sat at the end of this long peninsula in a town called, Asharoken. His house was a mansion and massive. Raine and Paul went together and, although they enjoyed the picnic, as well as confused when the rich bastard treated them as close and dear friends during the party, they wanted to see more of the area itself. They easily slipped away after only being there for less than an hour, jumped back into Paul's newly bought Mercedes convertible and went for a joy ride.

They went as far out as the road would lead, which was to the tip of the peninsula. Only a wide parking area existed at the end of it, surrounded by a rocky beach and the Long Island Sound which connected to the Atlantic Ocean. It was both barren and beautiful at the same time. Raine had stolen a bottle of their employer's best whiskey, Bushmill, and both sat on the hood of Paul's Mercedes where they drank, smoked whatever was left from a roach clip Paul had in his glove compartment, and bonded. It was the epitome of utter relaxation for both, and from that day on, they vowed to make it a point to get out there several times every year when the itch to get away from it all struck either of them, which they did. That was the one spot in the world where Raine felt he could completely be himself. And that's where they were heading now.

Raine pulled over and parked when he first turned on Eaton Neck Road, the stretch of land that led straight out to their favorite spot and the Long Island Sound. It was even darker out there, with no streetlights, so he left the car's headlights on.

"Why are you stopping?" asked Paul.

Raine turned to his friend. "Again, do you remember what you did in the bathroom before our first big meeting?"

Paul giggled and grinned as he lowered his chin to his chest. He was now in a silly mood, past the point of being boisterous and loud.

"Do you?" asked Raine, smiling.

"Yes," answered Paul. "Oh, my God! I was such a fucking idiot!" he shouted.

Raine began to laugh. "You wanted so badly to make a big impression, so you looked in the mirror fixing your fucking tie I don't know how many times. And then…"

"No!" shouted Paul, embarrassed.

"And then," Raine laughed, "You pulled out this fucking bottle of cologne…"

"Canoe!" shouted Paul.

"Yeah, fucking Canoe Cologne, and you began splashing that shit all over yourself. You smelled like you took a dive in a pool of it."

"My God, what in hell was I thinking?" Paul said rolling his head back on the seat's headrest.

"I don't now," Raine said, laughing. "But everyone could smell you a mile away. I mean, don't get me wrong, it smelled pretty good, but, man, it was a freakin' miracle we got that account."

Paul closed his eyes and shook his head. "I bought a bottle of that shit the night before. The sales girl, who was hot, by the way, told me the scent was a huge turn on."

"For a chick, yeah, but a room full of men?" Raine laughed.

"I don't know. Whatever," Paul said, lazily waving his hand. "Fucking Canoe."

Raine looked at his pal, and then leaned over and opened the glove compartment. He reached inside and pulled out the bottle of cologne. It was Canoe Cologne. He held it up to Paul.

"Oh, no fucking way! Are you fucking kidding me?" Paul shouted, grabbing the bottle and looking at it. "Where the fuck did you get this?"

"I found it in the car. I guess my father wore it," Raine lied.

"Holy shit," said Paul as he unscrewed the top and took a whiff. "Yup, that's it!" He held it out to Raine.

Raine took the bottle and took a whiff. He gave Paul a strange look, pretending as if he couldn't smell it, and then carefully removed the small cap that held the liquid inside and took another whiff. "Yeah, that's the smell," he said.

Then, as if by "accident," he tipped the bottle over, spilling a third of it all over Paul's shoulder and neck.

Paul jolted back. "What the fuck!" he cried.

"Oh, man, I'm sorry. Shit, I'm so sorry," Raine said, but he wasn't. This was the best smell he ever smelled, and now the car reeked of it. He never admitted to Paul that it was, and hid his aromatic delight.

"Jeez, now I'm gonna reek just like I did a hundred years ago," Paul said, half angry, half laughing.

"Let me make it up to you," said Raine as he pulled the keys from the ignition. "You drive."

"What?" asked Paul, liking the idea, but not sure he was up for the task.

"You drive, no one's around. Just put the brights on and take us all the way out," encouraged Raine, dangling the car keys in front of Paul's face.

"But I'm...still wasted," Paul moaned.

"Nah, you're good. We'll roll down the windows. That'll wake you up," assured Raine.

Paul looked at Raine, unsure, and then grinned a wide, mischievous grin. "OK. What the hell," he said as he snatched the keys from Raine's hand and jumped out of the car.

Raine opened his door and got out. They both passed each other giggling as they ran around the car to the other side. Raine got in the passenger seat and closed the door. Paul climbed into the driver's seat and closed his door. He wiped his neck, trying to get the cologne off him, but it was no use. It was there and would stay there until he got into a shower. He struggled to find the ignition, banging the car key into the side of the steering wheel several times before Raine helped guide it into its right place. Paul turned the key and the engine roared. Raine reached over and flipped the bright switch, making the headlights shine stronger than before.

"See? There's the road...clear as ever," Raine pointed ahead.

Paul smiled, put the car in drive and slowly pulled back on to the road. Raine pressed the button that rolled his window all the way down, and encouraged Paul to do the same. He did. The fresh air helped clear out the cologne reeked car a little, but not a lot. It also helped to clear Paul's head a bit as well.

At first Paul drove like an elderly person, slow and with great caution. He had both hands on the steering wheel and sat forward, staring at the road ahead as if he was trying to read small print. There was no one else on the road, but still, Paul was being paranoid and this was getting on Raine's nerves.

"Come on! Step on the gas," he told Paul.

"I...I don't want to crash," Paul muttered nervously, never taking his eyes off the road.

"Into what?" Raine asked. "A pile of sand?"

"I'm hungry," Paul announced out of the blue.

"You are?" Raine said with a grin. "OK, pull over."

Paul gave a quick glance to Raine, and then nervously put his eyes back on the road. "Pull over where? There's no place to eat out here."

"Just pull over," Raine insisted.

It took Paul a few minutes to slowly pull over to the side of the road where there was nothing but dirt and sand. The road was the only thing that was paved.

"Turn off the car," said Raine.

Paul obeyed. Raine reached over and pulled the

keys out of the ignition. "I'll be right back," he said as he hopped out of the car and went to the back.

Paul watched the trunk of the car go up momentarily, and then slam back down. Raine got back in the car holding the hoagie. He knew Paul always got hungry after a night of drinking. Raine closed his door and held it out to Paul. The aroma was immediately familiar to Paul.

"No way!" he said as a grin came across his face. "Are you fucking kidding me?"

"I picked it up earlier this evening," Raine said, smiling.

Paul went to grab it, but Raine held it back.

"Wait. I'll let you have it, but you have to promise to drive faster after you're done eating. Deal?"

Paul, without hesitation, said, "Deal," and then grabbed the hoagie and unwrapped it. The smell instantly made battle with the cologne that already had permeated the car. It was an odd mixture of delicatessen meets Macy's.

"God, I love that smell," said Raine, sitting back. He had a "best" smell, but it was that combination of Canoe Cologne, the hoagie, and salty sea air coming off the beach.

"Me, too," said Paul as he grabbed one half of the hoagie and handed the other to Raine. By this time, it was a soggy mess having been sitting in that strange oil for the last few hours. But neither cared, they ate it anyway. Raine ate slowly, savoring the scent and taste. Paul devoured his, as if he hadn't eaten in weeks. Since they had no napkins, they both used their expensive Italian suite jacket sleeves to wipe the crumbs and oil from their lips.

They sat back in silence as they ate, with only the sound of the ocean, wind and their munching heard. Raine didn't finish his half. He wasn't very hungry, but he ate a good portion of it. Seeing this, Paul asked if he could finish it for him, having already finished his. Raine was more than happy to hand it over. He liked seeing his friend enjoying something so simple and with such gusto.

When Paul was finished, he crumbled up the old wax paper, handed it to Raine and asked for the keys.

"You ready?" asked Raine, holding them away from Paul.

"I got food in me now, I'm fucking ready," said Paul, eager to get going.

Raine grinned and handed Paul the keys. It took only two tries this time for him to get the key in the ignition, but once he did, he flashed on the bright headlights, revved the engine and peeled out from the side of the road.

Paul swerved a lot as he sped down the long, dark stretch of road. There was nobody on it at that hour, so it was perfect to go way beyond the speed limit. Raine shouted for him to roll down all the windows, which Paul did, causing the sea salt air to whip wildly throughout the car. Both their hair blew back, and then sideways and then back again. Raine leaned his head back on the headrest, wearing a big smile. He had all of his three favorite smells going at once. The best part about it was he was racing into darkness at breakneck speed at the same time. Take that, tumor and death! He thought as the wind slapped his face. He never felt so alive.

"Music!" shouted Raine. "Where's the fucking

music?"

It was the only thing missing from this invigorating moment, so he sat forward and turned on the radio. It was still set on that station that played only 90's music. As soon as he turned it on, the happy, bouncy pop tune, "MMMBop" by Hanson had just begun. Raine turned up the volume way up.

"Oh, hell no!" shouted Paul.

"Oh, hell YES!" Raine shouted back.

Paul looked at Raine, surprised, when he heard him sing loudly along to the song and hung his head out of the window like a happy puppy. The hardcore Springsteen fan was singing along to Hanson, of all groups! The sight made Paul laugh so hard he began to swerve, but quickly pulled the car back in the correct lane. Raine nervously pulled his head back in. Laughing at this, Paul, too, began to sing along to the bubble gum pop song.

Both looked at each other surprised that they knew the lyrics, something they would never admit to anyone, and then laughed harder as they sang louder.

It had turned into the perfect night for Raine. He was as happy as the song. Happier then he could ever remember. He realized it was because he had finally let go.

CHAPTER TWENTY-NINE

RAINE AND PAUL MANAGED TO make it out to the end of the neck by the time the song ended, which was a little less than four minutes. That must be a record for those who are from that area. Paul drove into the dark, barren parking lot at the tip, where he's been so many times before, and spun the car around a few times before stopping. He turned off the car, opened his door and fell out laughing. Raine did the same.

It was cold out there, but neither felt it or cared. Their laughter echoed over the ocean around them, drifting over the winds and the waves, and hitting the rocks on all sides of them. Raine watched as Paul went to the front of the car, hopped up on the hood and laid spread eagle on top of it. The warmth from the engine felt good. Raine climbed up and did the same. They lied there, side by side, looking up at the stars for several moments in silence. The drive was exhilarating, but now they needed stillness and reflection.

Paul let out a heavy sigh and said, "You know, I want to say one more thing about Connie, and then put it behind me."

Raine said nothing, but his silence didn't mean he didn't want to talk about it.

Paul looked up at the sky and said, "I really thought she was the one. I invested my heart, you know? Shit, I've made so many investments with money, but that was different, and the most important. I lost. And I lost not only her, but my best friend. I'll never do that again."

Raine sat up and slid down a bit, resting his feet on the front bumper. "You have to know, she wasn't in love with me. And that night...I couldn't get it up."

Paul slowly lifted his body and leaned back on his elbows. "What?" he asked.

"Nothing happened that night. I was too envious of your promotion and felt...I don't know, I guess I felt inferior, or something. But what I do know is...nothing happened."

"You mean...but, wait, she told me she was in love with you," said Paul, confused.

"She told me she loved your cologne."

"What?"

Raine laughed. "She told me she loved your cologne. Canoe. She said you smelled better than I did, and after I couldn't, you know, perform, she said you were better at that, too. Man, I was there to build myself up and she just shot me down at every turn. It was a pretty bad night," he admitted and looked down at the pavement.

Paul looked out at the darkness, thinking, for several moments. He then quickly looked back at Raine.

"Wait…how the fuck would she know if I was better if she never did it with you?" he asked.

Raine was glad his back was to Paul so he couldn't see his eyes widened with guilt. He told him a lie to make his friend feel better, and now had to think of something quick. He turned and looked at Paul.

"How the hell should I know? But she was right about your cologne. That part was true."

Paul looked at Raine, confused, and then realized he was making all this up to make him feel better. Paul began to laugh.

"She loved my cologne," said Paul, shaking his head. "Nice try." He sat up and slid down to the edge of the hood next to Raine and slapped him on the back. "You're so full of shit, but I love ya anyway, Addison."

Raine grinned and hung his head down. They sat there for a moment saying nothing.

"Hey, do me a favor…" Paul began, breaking the silence.

"Name it."

"Promise me we'll stay in touch. Let's not lose touch again. I really missed you."

Raine didn't say a word, nor did he look up. He stared down at the pavement knowing he couldn't make that promise. It made him sad, so sad that he began to choke up, but didn't give in to his emotions. He bit his lower lip to make sure he didn't start to cry. Paul waited for an affirmation, and began to feel slighted.

"Hey…come on, Raine. Promise me we'll stay in touch. And not just for, like, a few weeks and then that's it. I'm talking about for life here. Promise me we'll be friends until the day we die."

Raine closed his eyes upon hearing this. He smiled because he knew for sure that was a promise he could definitely keep. Until the day we die. Raine slowly brought his head up and looked at Paul. "OK. I promise."

Paul threw his arm around Raine's shoulder and gave him a sideways hug. Then, suddenly, he moved his arm away and began to slowly slide off the hood. "Oh, man…"

"What's wrong?" Raine asked, concerned.

"I'm gonna hurl," Paul whimpered as he doubled over, covering his mouth and sprinted several yards away into the darkness.

Raine was about to follow until he heard the sound of projectile hitting the pavement. He winced, and then winced again when he heard Paul do it a second, third and fourth time. Maybe that hoagie wasn't such a good idea after all, he thought. He was glad he wasn't able to see his friend. Thank God for the darkness. He didn't worry about anything happening to Paul as long as he heard his exhausted moans echoing off the Long Island Sound. Raine slid off the hood, leaned on the car and waited until the worst had passed.

After about fifteen minutes, Paul staggered out from of the darkness, wiping his mouth on his sleeve. He was more sober now, but looked like a train had hit him. He nearly tripped at one point, but steadied himself.

"Oh, jeez…what a mess," groaned Paul.

"The seagulls will clean it up," Raine said with a laugh.

Paul put both hands on the hood of the car and

leaned forward. "I think I'm gonna pass out, man. I'm sorry."

"Let's go. We've had enough for one night," said Raine as he grabbed hold of Paul's shoulders, helped him to stand erect and led him around the car. He opened the passenger side door and got him safely in the seat.

Raine closed the door, and then, as he made his way around to the driver's side, he paused momentarily and looked up at the black sky where little stars twinkled in the distance. He closed his eyes, inhaled deeply a few times to try to suck in all he could of the moment, his very last at this, his favorite spot in the world, and then got into the car.

"Go to sleep," he said to Paul as he took hold of the keys in the ignition. "I'll wake you know when we get to Brooklyn."

But Paul was way ahead of him. He had passed out the second he sat down. Raine looked at him and smiled. He started the car, and then slowly found his way back on that long road home.

CHAPTER THIRTY

RAINE THOUGHT ABOUT A LOT of things during his drive back into the city, especially about how fleeting time was. It had only been a short while ago that he was sharing a hoagie with Paul on the side of the road, but now it seemed like a hundred years had passed since. It was weird, he thought, how life was like that. Nothing was permanent.

Too bad, he thought. God should have created a better system to make good times last a little longer. Raine chuckled after he thought that. Who was he to tell God, or whatever, how to run things? If there was a God, Raine found himself hoping He wouldn't hold a grudge against his arrogance, and for a lot of other things he had done during his short life.

He looked over at Paul, and then back at the road. Tears started to form in his eyes when he tried to imagine what his friend would look like in twenty years. By that time, Paul will be fifty-three and have grey hair, and maybe a wife and some kids. Raine wondered what Paul's kids would be like. He wondered if Paul would share stories with his wife about their friendship, or if he'd remember him at all. He was grateful that he had that night with Paul. Paul was definitely someone with whom he regretted most strongly falling out with. He wished he had contacted Paul sooner, but he knew it wasn't his way. Raine was a different person then. He let out a slight chuckle thinking how "then" was only a couple of weeks ago. Man, time was a funny thing...a weird, fucked up, funny thing.

Raine grew tired of his thoughts. They were getting too heavy and morose, so he turned on the radio with the volume low. The music would keep him company. He appreciated that a Jackson Browne song came on. He liked Jackson Browne, and wondered why he didn't have any of his stuff in his collection. A huge oversight on his part, Raine admitted to himself. He would definitely buy everything Jackson Browne ever recorded now if only he had the time. He then made a mental note to ask April if she had any. He was sure she did.

The song on the radio was "Sky Blue and Black," and the lyrics strangely fit exactly Raine's thoughts and mood. Jackson Browne is a genius, he thought to himself as he turned it up just a little more so he could hear it better. He looked at Paul to see if the music would stir him, but Paul was dead to the world. Temporarily dead, that is, Raine thought. Paul had a good, long life ahead of him.

Jackson Browne's melody and words filled Raine with a feeling of hope and ease he hadn't felt since he started his strange journey. Although the lyrics were somewhat sad, they made him think of April and the message he wanted to leave her. He leaned his right elbow on the door, tilted his head and ran his hand through his hair. No matter what, she would be okay, he thought. Yes, everything would be okay, he reassured himself as he sat back, comfortable in his seat. Everything was going to really be okay.

•••••

It was nearing 3am by the time Raine got Paul out of the car and up into his brownstone. He found Paul's keys in his jacket pocket, got Paul and himself inside and clumsily dragged Paul to the couch. That was as far as he could make it since Paul was still passed out and was too difficult to carry. He flopped him down, and lifted his feet off the floor, making sure he was in a good sleeping position. Raine then carefully untied Paul's shoes, removed them, and then covered his feet and his entire body with a throw blanket he found on a nearby chair.

Raine moved over to Paul's chest and loosened his tie. He didn't want him to choke, not that he would, but he wanted to make sure. He also unbuttoned the first two buttons of Paul's shirt. Raine then stood and looked at his friend sleeping soundly. Paul was going to feel a terrible hangover in the morning, Raine thought, as he stepped back and sat down in a chair across from him.

He watched the rhythmic breathing of Paul's chest, and studied his face. He didn't want to forget a single thing about the guy with whom he always deemed the brother he never had. Paul was the man Raine hoped he would have become. Honest, good-natured and smart without having to screw anybody over. He was glad he knew Paul. He was right there, all along, to show him the best way on how to maneuver his way through life, but Raine was too proud and arrogant to see it. Now he did, and he didn't want to forget it.

"I'm going to miss you, buddy," said Raine in a soft, sincere voice. "I know you can't hear me, and maybe that's why I can talk to you like this now." Raine took a deep breath and let it out. "I'm dying, Paul. I have a brain tumor that they can't do anything about. I only have a few weeks left, maybe more. Who knows? But time doesn't matter anymore because it's going to pass along anyway and move forward without me."

Raine's own words hit him hard. His lips began to quiver as he fought back tears. "Paul...I'm scared. I'm scared shitless, and there's nothing I can do about it." He lowered his head and began to sob. He held his head down for a long while, before he slowly looked up again.

"I'm glad I knew you, Paul. Thank you for being my friend. Thanks for seeing past my bullshit and believing that I was still good enough to spend time with. I sure as hell didn't deserve it, but I really appreciated it."

Raine slowly stood, wiped his tears, took in a deep breath and then let it out. He reached into his pocket and pulled out his last envelope. He looked at it, and then realized he needed a pen. He went over to a desk in the corner of the room, opened a drawer and found one. He wrote a short message on envelope, asking Paul to wait thirty days before opening it, and then went over to the coffee table and carefully placed it against a book so Paul wouldn't miss it.

Raine looked down at his friend one last time, said

softly, "Goodbye, Paul," and then he quietly left.

CHAPTER THIRTY-ONE

RAINE DIDN'T BOTHER TO TURN on the radio as he drove over the Brooklyn Bridge and back into Manhattan. He wanted some quiet time. He saw on the dashboard clock that it was now 4:30am. He knew he could be home in Connecticut within an hour, easily, but there was one more stop he needed to make, so he made his way through the empty New York City streets and headed for his office building.

It was an eerie feeling to pull into the vacant parking structure beneath his building. Raine had never seen it so bare before. He parked in the spot that still had his name on it. A reminder that he needed to take care of that, and wondered who would end up getting this sliver of prime New York City parking.

When he stepped out of the car, he had no feeling in his feet. This caused him to lose his balance, but thankfully he was close to the car and was able to hold on to it before falling. Both his feet were completely numb and this frightened him. He leaned on the car and shook one leg violently, hoping this would bring the feeling back. It didn't. He then stomped his foot on the hard concrete several times. He was grateful no one was around to see this, and even looked up at the corners of the parking garage to see if any cameras were on him. He thankfully didn't see any, and put his attention back on his feet.

He shook his other leg, and then stomped his foot again, to no avail. He wondered if he should get back in his car and go back to Connecticut. But he was already inside the building and he needed to get up to his office. Damn it, he thought, angry at his situation. He stomped both his feet once again for another five minutes until suddenly, he felt a strange tingling return to his toes. He sighed relief when the sensation turned into real feeling again. Within a few minutes both feet were back to normal. Damn this tumor, Raine thought as he quickly made his way to the elevator and got inside.

The hum of the elevator was louder than he remembered, but it was ridiculously early in the morning, so he didn't mind it, but he wanted off as soon as possible. Once the elevator reached his floor, he got off and headed down the short hall to his office suite. He remembered to bring his key card, which he swiped over the electronic security box. The door made a 'click' sound, and he entered.

Although it had only been a few weeks since he'd been away, the office felt different. Yes, everything was still in its place, but it felt cold and uninviting. It also felt empty. Of course, it was empty, with only a few of the overhead, fluorescent lights on which gave it an ominous feeling. Still, it was a different kind of emptiness, and Raine knew what that feeling meant. He was no longer a part of this company, and that fact stung at his heart.

The sense of dying was now more real than it had ever been. It was an unexpected sense, too. Somewhere in his head he thought being back in his office would make what was happening to him seem a really bad dream. That's what he was hoping for, but what he got made him both sad and scared at the same time. What worried him more was that it wasn't a feeling he could easily shake off. It was real.

Raine hurried down the hall to his office. His door was closed, but not locked. He was glad about that, but also annoyed. His office should always be locked, and thought for a quick moment to let Jennifer know this. But just as that thought came, the fact of it no longer mattering snuck up and made him dismiss it.

Raine was surprised to see his office intact when he entered. Except for the several contracts and papers for him to sign that were laid out on his desk, everything else was the same. He wasn't sure why this surprised him. Perhaps he thought they would have moved on without him by now and someone new had taken over. But that's how Raine thought. That's what would have happened if Raine were in charge. Screw the guy when he's flat on his back.

It strangely surprised Raine to realize that his colleagues didn't think, or work, in that way. Wow, he thought. Although he knew it, and had been repeatedly reminded of it during the past few days, it was still shocking for him to get that he really was an asshole.

He made his way around his desk, turned on the

lamp, and looked at the papers. Jennifer had pasted red arrow stickers on each contract to make it easy for him to see where to sign. Everything was laid out to perfection. She definitely was efficient, Raine thought. Something he never gave her credit for. In fact, he never gave he credit for anything.

A twinge of guilt and self-hate shot through him at the thought of this. Was it his power and position that made him such a prick, or was it something just innately in him? He wondered. No, he was definitely a prick, he silently decided to himself. No use denying what was true. He wasn't proud of it, but at least for the rest of his life he would be honest.

Raine looked over the contracts, but didn't sign them. He'd leave that for the next guy. Instead, he turned on his computer and opened up a Word document. He sat back in his leather chair that swerved smoothly at the slightest move, and began to think. Thankfully, his concentration was still intact, and his focus laser sharp. That was necessary as he began to figure out how best to compose his letter of resignation.

He didn't want the letter to be anything but professional, straight and to the point. However, he did want to leave his colleagues with some sort of pearl of wisdom, and maybe a thank you, but his mind went blank when it came to that sort of stuff. Plus, he could feel his anger start to build that he was being forced to write such a letter. He was only thirty-three years old.

He pounded his fist on the desk, angry that his life was being yanked away so unfairly, but then quickly composed himself. It was no use getting angry now. That wasn't going to change a damn thing. Just write the fucking letter, he thought, and get the hell out of there. And with that, he pulled his chair forward and began to type.

The words came surprisingly easy. He began by stating that he was resigning and explained why. He thought to just end it there, but then a strange thing happened. He addressed each of his colleagues personally and wrote several lines thanking them for their support. He even added a personal message about what they meant to him. It was odd because he did this not to have them think better of him, but because he meant it.

He was sincere when he wrote to Stein that he was sorry they never hung out together outside the office, or went to a Yankee game. How easily that would have been for the both of them to do. A wasted opportunity to create a friendship, Raine wrote.

To Anderson he expressed how he admired his ability to speak honestly and genuinely to clients. This was the key that brought in the most sought after businesses. Just by being himself, Anderson was well liked and respected. Raine didn't understand how that worked, which is why he couldn't let his guard down. He freely admitted that in the letter. It was the first time he ever actually did let his guard down…and if felt good.

He addressed several other colleagues in the same way. Regretting not taking time to get to know them better, spending too much time making money. He even addressed the staff in general, and apologized for being a douche bag. Yes, he actually wrote the words, "douche bag." Because that's what he was. He asked them all not to hold it against him, but added that he could understand if they still did.

He made a request at the end of the letter not to feel pity for him, but instead to take time to get to know each other. A business doesn't have to be cut throat. Enjoy life, he stated, you never know when it will be taken away from you.

Raine sat back and carefully looked over at what he had written. He didn't want to change a thing. He then looked at the clock on the wall. It was now 5:45am. He stood, walked around his desk and went over to his printer that was in the corner of the room. He was pleased to see the tray was full when he pulled it out. Again, Jennifer was diligent. He smiled as he shoved the tray back into its slot and went back over to his desk. He took out a directory of the office to count how many copies he needed to make. He wanted to make sure everyone got one. When he tallied the number, he entered it into the computer, pressed print and sat down to wait for the copies to come out.

He suddenly felt weary, so he faced his desk, folded his arms on it and rested his head down. It felt good to take a moment to relax. He had been through a lot in one week, and now that it was over, he was ready to do this one last thing before leaving his office for good.

He knew he would miss his desk…and his office…and the view behind him…and his life. If only he was able to do it all over again, he thought. If only he had…

"Mr. Addison?" came a voice from across the room.

Raine quickly lifted his head and saw Jennifer standing in the doorway wearing a jacket with a bag over her shoulder and holding a coffee.

"Jennifer! What are you doing here? It's…" Raine

began as he glanced up at the clock, "six in the morning."

"I know. Since you've been gone, Stanson has me working for him now, as well as overseeing your work. It's hard to keep up, so I come in early now to stay ahead." She took several steps into the office. "Are you all right? Are you coming back?"

Raine motioned for her to come closer to his desk. Jennifer stepped forward.

"I'm resigning," he said bluntly. "I'm printing out my resignation letter now."

Jennifer glanced over her shoulder at the printer, and then looked back at Raine, surprised. "You're leaving? Why?"

Raine relaxed back in his chair and spoke freely and honestly. "I have a brain tumor," he began.

Jennifer gasped.

"Yeah, a brain tumor. Anyway, it's inoperable and they gave me a few weeks to live," he said freely. He no longer cared who knew about it.

"Oh, my God, Mr. Addison. Th-that's awful," said Jennifer covering her mouth as tears welled in her eyes.

Raine was taken by her reaction. "Are you crying?" he asked, surprised.

Jennifer quickly wiped her tears, as if it was unprofessional. "I-I'm sorry. It's just…this is so terrible."

Raine sat forward. "Wow. I never thought I'd get any tears out of this. I've been such a dick to you."

Jennifer let out a short laugh and said, "True, but you're still human. And you're so young. I mean…I mean, God, this is terrible. I'm so sorry."

"Yeah, it sucks," said Raine, slowly growing

uncomfortable. "So, look, I'm glad you're here because I want to ask you something."

Jennifer nodded quickly, as if ready to do anything Raine asked of her.

"Do you like your job?

Jennifer looked at him, thrown. "Do I like my job? Yeah, I guess. It pays really well."

"So, you like the job because it pays really well?" asked Raine.

"It helps me to afford living here," answered Jennifer with a slight chuckle.

"OK, let me understand this…you only work here because it pays really well and it allows you to live in the city," Raine clarified.

"Well, yeah," said Jennifer.

"OK, so let me ask you again…do you like your job?"

"You mean what I do here every day?"

Raine nodded. Jennifer's eyes glanced to her left, and then to her right. Was this a trick question? She wondered. Or, was this some sick joke he was pulling? What if he wasn't really dying and this was just his way of finding a way to fire her? She was utterly confused. He did look like shit, she reasoned. It actually looked as if he hadn't slept in days, and maybe drunk. She chose her answer carefully.

"Yes. I like working here," she lied.

Raine stared at her, and then sat back in his chair. "You're such a liar, Jennifer. And a bad one, you know that?"

"No, no. I really do like working here," Jennifer

insisted.

"Stop it. You hate it. Be honest," Raine said. He looked at her and saw she was mixed up. Her expression was utter fear and confusion. He quickly relaxed and spoke to her in a soft, sincere tone. "Look, I am dying. This isn't a joke, OK? And I'm sorry that I've been such an asshole to you. When I think about it now, it makes me sick. I'm ashamed of it, actually. No one should treat anyone the way I've treated you. Like you were beneath me, and snapping at you like a Nazi. Jeez…I'm surprised you lasted as long as you did."

Jennifer began to speak, but Raine lifted his hand at her to not say a word. "I know. I get it. You put up with it because you needed the job to survive in New York. Yada, yada, yada. OK. Well, now that we're being honest here…we are being honest here, right?" he asked.

Jennifer nodded, although she still looked confused.

"Good. So tell me what you would love to do if you didn't need the money to survive in New York?"

"What I'd do?" asked Jennifer.

"Yeah. I mean I doubt very much that you had dreams of working in a large, sterile financial firm under a tyrant like me when you were a kid. And if you did, well, that's just fucked up."

Jennifer chuckled. "No, I didn't dream that," she said, letting down her guard. "I always wanted to cook. I mean, bake. I love to bake. That's what I do on weekends. I try different recipes with my mom. It relaxes me…helps me to forget this place for a little while."

Raine smiled. Finally, the truth was out. "I know that's what you love to do."

Jennifer shot him a surprised look. "You do?"

"Yeah. Last year at the company picnic you made those little lemon bar things. I ate about a dozen of them. They were good," said Raine.

Jennifer felt touched. He remembered her cookies? "You really liked them?" she asked.

"Well, yes and no. I mean, sure, they tasted good, but about thirty minutes later they gave me the runs, so I had to spend about twenty minutes in the freakin' port-a-potty."

Jennifer felt bad. "Oh," she said, looking embarrassed.

"And while I was in there, I overheard a conversation you had with that Lisa girl in acquisitions."

Jennifer's face froze in horror. "Y-you overheard us?"

"Yeah. I guess you thought no one was around. You two snuck behind the port-a-potty and talked about how much you hated your jobs, the picnic and especially me," Raine told her.

"Oh, God," said Jennifer, suddenly feeling queasy.

Raine looked up at the ceiling, recalling. "Let's see, I remember you called me a 'piece of shit,' and a 'dick on wheels,' and compared me to a terrorist. I mean, OK, I agree I'm the first two, but a terrorist? Really?"

"I-I'm sorry. I really am. I had no idea you were in there," said Jennifer nervously.

"Don't worry about it," said Raine, waving his hand. "It took my mind off of what was happening to me in that john. And it was well deserved…except the terrorist remark. I'm not that bad."

Jennifer looked down, embarrassed.

"Look, the point is, aside from all that, I heard you talking about how much you love to cook. Or bake. Or, whatever you call it. It was the first time I heard you talk about something so passionately. Actually, it was the only time I'd heard you speak at all since I've never given you any time to do it here. So, that's how I know how much you love to bake…and how much you despise being here."

"Am I fired?" asked Jennifer, nervously.

Raine looked at her, surprised. She obviously was still afraid of him, and thought the last thing he would do before leaving…and dying…was fire her. He felt a deep shame for making this girl so miserable.

"Yes," he said bluntly. "You are."

Tears began to well up in Jennifer's eyes. "I-I'm sorry, Mr. Addison. Truly, I am. I didn't know you were in that port-a-potty. I didn't mean to say those things. I really need this job, I need the money," she begged.

"I'm doing you a favor, Jennifer," he told her. "No one should work at a job they hate, or ignoring what they really love to do. Have you ever heard of the Culinary Institute of America? It's supposedly the best cooking school in the country. There's one upstate near Hyde Park."

"Yeah," answered Jennifer, still confused.

"You have? Good. Well, I think you need to go there. Get out of this job and get yourself in that school."

Jennifer let out a snide chuckle. "I'd love that, but a school like that costs around…"

"A hundred grand, maybe more, for full tuition," said Raine. "That includes dorm, books, etc."

"Yeah. I don't make nearly that much," said

Jennifer.

"I know," Raine said as he opened one of the drawers of his desk and removed a small set of keys. He leaned down, unlocked the bottom one, took out a medium-sized metal box and placed it on top of the desk. He then found another key on the key chain and opened it.

He stood, reached in and began taking out small stacks of cash. He lined them up side by side on his desk. There were six stacks in all. Raine looked at Jennifer. "There it is, one hundred and twenty-five thousand dollars. Now you can afford it."

"What?" asked Jennifer stunned.

"There's your tuition…for the school. Enroll, get yourself up to Hyde Park and learn how to make lemon bars that won't give people the freakin' runs!"

Jennifer felt floored, and became speechless. She quickly moved closer to the desk, put her coffee on the edge of it, slipped her bag off her shoulder, put it on a chair, and then began to make her way around toward Raine.

"Oh, Mr. Addison…"

"Stop! Stop. Don't. No hugs. Get back where you were," he commanded.

She obeyed, and went back to where she was standing.

"Sorry. I didn't mean to order you like that, but I'm not a, you know, touchy feeling kind of guy."

"I understand," said Jennifer. "But Mr. Addison, I really don't know what to say?"

"Just say you'll do it."

"I want to, but…well, it's my mother. I kind of

support her, and if I go up to Hyde Park…I can't leave her."

Raine let out a frustrated sigh. He reached into the metal box and took out three more stacks of money and placed them with the rest. "There. That's a hundred and seventy-five grand. That should get you through school, and nice place up there for you and your mom. Will that do? Wait, screw it," he said reaching into the box and pulling out two more stacks. "OK, there, two hundred grand. I don't have anything left in the box. That's all I got. Take it or leave it."

Jennifer's eyes bulged. "I-I'll take it. I'll take it. Thank you so much, Mr. Addison."

"You've earned it," said Raine sincerely. "Now, there is just one last thing I want you to do for me. A big favor."

"Name it. Anything," said Jennifer, eagerly.

"Do you know how to make a cake? A good one?"

"Yeah. Cakes I can make," she said confidently.

"Good, because my sister will be getting married in a few months, and she'll need a nice cake. I want you to make one for her, for the wedding. I'm sure you have all the information about when it is, and where, since you've been privy to all those emails from her that I've stupidly ignored."

Jennifer sadly nodded. Her immense joy suddenly shattered by why Raine was being so kind to her. She tried not to cry, knowing he disliked it so much.

"Are you any good with wedding cakes?" he asked.

Jennifer smiled. "Actually, I am. I took a wedding cake and decorating class last year. I was the best in the class. So, yeah, I can totally do it. And I will. I want to."

"Good. April will appreciate that. You can call her after I'm…" Raine began to say, but stopped himself. "You know. Find out what she wants."

Jennifer swallowed hard. "OK," she said softly. "I will."

Raine put the cash back in the metal box, and then locked it and handed it to Jennifer along with the key. Jennifer's hands shook when she took it from him.

"Take a cab home with that. You don't want to lose it on the subway."

"Oh, no. I sure don't," said Jennifer.

"I've already sent an email to my attorney letting him know that I am giving you cash for the school. I'll phone him later to let him know how much. I don't want anyone bothering you about it. It's yours free and clear."

"Oh, thank you so much, Mr. Addison," Jennifer said holding out her hand.

Raine looked at it. He slowly took her hand and shook it. It was the first time they had ever made any sort of physical contact, although he wished he had been able to feel the softness of her skin, but his hand was numb again. He didn't tell her this, but felt life was being unfairly cruel with him in that moment. The one time he had left to finally connect with this young woman he so shabbily treated, and now came to respect and like.

Raine pulled his hand away and said, "The sun's coming up. I need to get out of here before people start arriving. Do me a favor," he said as he began shutting down his computer, "take the letters in the printer and put one on each executive desk and into the entire staff's mailboxes. Then go to your desk, write one of your own to Stanson. Be honest, tell him he's a dick… and then walk out the door, and never, ever come back. OK?"

"OK," said Jennifer wearing a big smile.

Raine looked at her, and tilted his head in appreciation.

"What?" Jennifer asked, suddenly feeling self-conscience.

"It's the first time I've ever seen you smile. You have a nice smile."

Jennifer blushed. Raine held his gaze for just a moment longer, and then grabbed his keys, made his way around his desk past Jennifer and headed for the door.

"Mr. Addison…" Jennifer called out. Raine stopped and turned around. "Take care of yourself…and thank you. You've changed my life."

Raine smiled, nodded, and then left the room.

Jennifer stood there for a moment, still trying to comprehend everything that had just taken place. She slowly took a seat, put her hands on the metal box, hung her head down and began to weep. As she did this, Raine, having forgotten something, appeared at the doorway. He stopped short before entering, seeing Jennifer crying.

Jennifer didn't know he was there. If she had, she probably wouldn't have prayed out loud through her tears, "Please, God, take care of Mr. Addison. Please save him. If that's not possible, please don't let him be in too much pain."

This stunned and moved Raine. Hearing someone praying for him touched his soul like nothing else ever had, especially from someone with whom he had been so cruel and callous toward. He lowered his head for a moment in deep appreciation and gratitude before he no longer cared what he came back for and quietly stepped away from the doorway.

The request Jennifer made to God swum around in Raine's mind as he rode the elevator down to the parking garage. He hadn't given much thought about God, but hearing Jennifer talk so directly to this invisible entity made him wonder if He was real.

When the elevator doors opened, Raine stepped out feeling confident. All he had set out to do was now finished. There was no one else to see, no more tasks to complete. It had been a short journey, yet the most meaningful he had ever taken. He was ready to go, he affirmed to himself. Not just home to Connecticut, but to leave his life. He was grateful for having the time to do what he needed to do, and quietly thanked God Himself for giving it to him.

Raine climbed into his father's Lexus and pulled out of his parking spot for the last time. He drove through the empty garage and out on to the street. It was now close to 7am. The sun was still rising, and cast long, beautiful shadows on the streets. A new day, Raine thought, and there would be many more to come, with or without him. Life indeed does goes on.

As Raine drove through the New York City streets, heading for Connecticut, he didn't turn on the radio. Instead, he rolled down all the windows in the car so he could hear the well-orchestrated sounds of the city. It would be the last time he'd have this opportunity and he wanted to take full advantage of it. He felt oddly lucky knowing he would never drive through that town again. And because it was the last time, it made him keenly aware of all his surroundings.

He suddenly didn't care anymore about dying. He was glad that it gave him the chance to deeply appreciate everything. Why, he wondered, didn't everyone do this every day while they had the chance? He shook his head and silently began to mourn the living.

CHAPTER THIRTY-TWO

One month later.

APRIL SPENT A FULL WEEK planning Raine's funeral. She was thankful he went peacefully, and it happened very close to how Doctor Katz had predicted. His hearing was the first to go. His sense of taste the second. His sense of feeling and smell soon followed, and lastly was his sight, but by that time he was slipping in and out of comas. It all happened swiftly, all in a span of a week. Prior to that, Raine had a good and healthy two weeks to spend with his sister in which they shared a lot and gained closure on many things.

During that time, Raine allowed himself to be an open book for April. He didn't want to leave her needing anything. Financially she was secure, but more important, emotionally. And in return, she was there at his side, holding his hand when he passed to make sure her brother did not die alone the way he had lived.

The day of the funeral was tough on April. Guy was

at her side the entire time, but not his presence, or his strong arm to which she clung, took away her deep feelings of emptiness and loss. She still bemoaned how it should have been her to go first, and how "little time" there was. It was all so unfair.

There were many people at the church that day, however, almost all were April's friends, as well as Guy's. They were there to rally and show support, knowing the pain she was experiencing. But there were a spattering of Raine's colleagues. A handful of executives in business suits that looked uncomfortable and out of place. But they were there, and their attendance at least showed they had some respect for their fallen associate. They each introduced themselves to April in a brief and awkward manner, which reminded her of how Raine was when he first arrived at her home a month earlier. Stoic and distant with a hint of forced kindness. She was very grateful that they came, but felt sorry for them in a strange way and secretly hoped, minus the pain or suffering he endured, that they would discover what her brother had before he left the earth.

It was moments before the service was to begin when Louise Gardner arrived. She was in her nun habit and looked lovely. She stood in the back of the church in search of April. April was standing in the middle aisle, talking with a friend when she turned her head and looked over at Louise. They both locked eyes at the same time, and knew instantly just on instinct, who the other one was. April excused herself and quickly made her way to Louise.

"Sister Louise?" she asked putting out her hand to greet her.

"Yes. April?"

April nodded. They shook hands and embraced.

"I'm so glad you came," said April.

"I am happy to be here. How are you doing?" Louise asked.

April sighed. "OK…considering. He went peacefully. No pain at the end."

Louise nodded with a sad expression. "I hope we can spend some time after to talk."

"Oh, yes, I'd like that very much," said April, eagerly happy for the opportunity.

Just then, a low, nervous sounding voice came up from behind Louise. "Excuse me…are you April?"

April peered over Louise's shoulder. Louise stepped aside. It was George Doit. He was there with his mother. He was withdrawn and wore an old suit that looked almost one size too big for him. He had stubble on his face from lack of a good razor, but he was standing and talking, a far cry from sitting nearly comatose in a mental ward.

"Yes," responded April, unsure.

"M-my name is George Doit. Raine and I were friends. We went to college together."

April's face lit up. She looked at Louise. Louise smiled. April stepped toward George and took his hand.

"Hello, it's so nice to meet you," April said, surprised to be in the company of an actual friend of her brother's.

George recoiled a little from her touch, but stayed present. He managed a slight smile, and then, diverting the attention from himself, gently pulled his hand away and introduced his mother. His mother quickly stepped forward and shook April's hand.

"I'm sorry for your loss. It happened so fast. I wish I had known Raine longer. He was such a sweet young man. We had tea at my house just a few weeks ago. Strange how life works, right?" she asked. Her tone was a bit abrasive, but that was just her way from being alone in her house for so long.

"You had tea with Raine?" asked April, perplexed.

"Yeah. He came to the house looking for George, but George was in the hospital," she told her, as George lowered his head, embarrassed that his mother was so free in giving out personal information.

"Oh, right," said April. "The hospital. I heard about that."

"We both liked Raine very much, and George insisted we come today to pay our respects. He got special permission to from his doctor. They were so impressed that he made the request himself that they said OK. Of course, he needed a chaperone."

George shook his head, again embarrassed by his mother's need to share every detail. April took George's hand and held it. George looked up at her.

"You have no idea how much your being here means to me," she said with tears in her eyes.

Touched by her kindness, George asked, "Can I...I mean, do you think it would be all right if...I could say something today?"

"You want to speak about Raine?" April asked surprised.

George nodded. "It won't be much, but I'd like to."

April was now deeply moved. She looked at Louise,

who gave a slight nod. "Why, yes. That would be lovely," she sighed happily. "Raine would have liked that very much."

George smiled for the first time. He then quickly looked down at the floor again. April put her hand to her chest to signify how very touched she was by this and looked at Louise. Louise smiled as she reached out and stroked April's arm.

At that moment, Claude and Jimmy entered the church. They glanced around, looking curious and confused. April saw them and wondered who they were, and if they had accidentally miscalculated the regular mass services. Claude saw April, and since they made eye contact, he walked over to her with Jimmy right behind him.

"Pardon," he said to April in his thick French accent. "We are looking for…" he stopped momentarily, pulled out a piece of paper from his jacket pocket and read, "April Addison."

"I'm April," she said, perplexed.

Claude smiled. He looked at Jimmy who was smiling, too, as he eyed April. They both looked relieved and happy to have found her.

"My name is Claude Meunier, and this is Shimeee Dufour. We knew your brother, Raine, and wanted to come to pay our respects."

Jimmy smiled as he held out his hand to shake April's. She shook it, and then Claude did the same. April looked at them confused, yet happy to have them there.

"H-how did you know my brother?" she asked.

"He came to our restaurant several weeks ago to

have what he considered his best food. Eggs Benedict," answered Claude with a grin.

April chuckled. "Oh, that's right. His list. Yours was his favorite taste. Eggs Benedict!" April said with a slight roll of her eyes.

"I know!" exclaimed Claude. "We have a restaurant in Baltimore…"

"Baltimore?" said April, surprised.

"Oui, and your brother drove out from New Jersey in the middle of the night just to have my eggs Benedict. Bah! If I had known really what this was all about, I would have made him the most exquisite dinner on the menu," Claude told her.

"No, Claude," Jimmy said, stepping forward. "The man wanted eggs Benedict. Nothing more, and you gave it to him. You made him very, very happy."

"Oui. Oui," said Claude nodding his head in agreement. "In any case, we are most sorry you have lost your brother. He was a very, very kind man."

"Thank you. But how did you know about…" April began to ask when suddenly she saw Paul Winston entered the church. He looked familiar, but April couldn't place the face or how she knew him. "Excuse me a moment," she said as she walked away from Claude, Jimmy, Louise, George and his mother.

"Hello," April said to Paul as she approached him.

"Hi," said Paul. "Am I too late?"

"No, we haven't started yet. Do we know each other?" asked April.

"Oh, I'm sorry. Yeah, we do…sort of. I'm Paul Winston. We met…God, I hate to say it…at your parent's funeral."

April looked at him, trying to remember.

"I was working with Raine at the Russell Company in New York. We came up together."

"Oh, that's right," said April. "The two of you were very close."

"Well, for a while there, yeah, but then we had kind of a falling out. I just saw Raine a few weeks ago. Thankfully we patched things up before...jeez, I had no idea he was…" Paul began to say, but then stopped himself.

"He didn't want anyone to know," said April with a sigh.

"Yeah. Typical Addison."

"How did you hear about his passing?" asked April, curious.

"Oh, he wrote me this letter," said Paul as he began to reach into his vest pocket.

At that moment, Mrs. Shapiro entered the church. She was dressed conservatively yet looked lovely. April recognized her immediately. She excused herself from Paul momentarily to greet her.

"Mrs. Shapiro?" asked April as she approached her and they shook hands.

"Yes. Hello, April. I'm glad you remember me," Mrs. Shapiro said with a sad smile.

"Of course. You were Raine's favorite teacher. I'm so touched that you came. Raine would have loved your being here," admitted April.

"Well, it was by his request," she said with a tone that sounded bittersweet.

April looked at her confused. "His request?"

"Yes. He came to visit me several weeks ago. He didn't tell me that he was dying, but we spent a little time together, and before he left he handed me an envelope and asked me to wait a month before I opened it. I had no idea what was inside, but did as he requested. He wrote me the kindest letter, so of course I had to come."

"May I ask what was in the letter?"

Mrs. Shapiro opened her purse and pulled out the envelope. She opened it and handed the letter to April. April read it silently. Tears welled up in her eyes as she did this. She sniffled a few times before finishing it.

"I...I can't believe it. I mean...I can't believe he did this," said April as she turned and looked over at the others who were now standing in a small group holding the same letter and talking among themselves.

April slowly made her way toward the group. Mrs. Shapiro followed.

"You all...got the same letter?" April asked them.

"Looks like it," said Paul. "Except we all were different "bests" for Raine. When it came to smell, I was the best he ever experienced."

"Mine was the best taste," chimed in Claude, holding up his letter.

"I was the best thing he ever heard," said George, holding his letter.

Mrs. Shapiro stepped forward. "I was his best touch."

"And I was his best sight," Louise said, hoping no one would wonder, or ask about it.

Just then, Guy approached the group and stood next to April. "Honey, they're ready to begin," he said gently.

April was too overwhelmed with sadness and appreciation to move. As Guy tried to lead her away, she hesitated and handed Guy Mrs. Shapiro's letter. Guy looked at the small gathering confused, and then silently read the letter. A look of respect and warm regret brought tears to his eyes. The group watched as he folded the letter, handed it back to April and embraced her. April began to cry.

Claude stepped forward and gently touched her shoulder. "We are all here for you."

As the others murmured in agreement, April pulled away from Guy and wiped her tears.

"Are you OK?" Guy asked.

"Yes. I'll be all right. Come on, everyone," April said, keeping a brave face.

As they all filed into the church and took their seats, April asked Mrs. Shapiro if she could "borrow" the letter Raine had written, promising to give it back to her after the service.

"It's yours," answered Mrs. Shapiro, squeezing April's arm, and then entered a pew and sat down.

The service began with an older priest, a friend of April and Guy's, speaking about life and death as he stood before Raine's casket. He then read two short passages from the Bible.

After that, Guy stood and spoke about Raine in an honest, humorous way. He told about his dislike for Raine initially, but then how he grew to respect his bravery through such a terrible illness. He also spoke about how Raine never complained, and was more concerned about his sister than himself. Above all, he knew Raine loved

April and did his best to show her that. Guy's words made April weep, as well as everyone else. He ended by calling Raine his "brother," and said farewell as he looked at the casket.

After Guy, it was George's turn. He walked slow and awkwardly up the few short steps to the altar. When he reached the podium, he stood and stared at the casket for a long while, as if he was in a trance. The guests grew a little uncomfortable and shot glances at each another, concerned. George's mother sat restless in her seat, worried. Maybe this wasn't a good idea after all. She looked over at April in a near panic, but April put up her hand and calmed her with a short motion of it.

George finally took his eyes off the casket and looked out at the guests. He let out a heavy sigh, and then began to speak. His words came out slow and methodical, yet they sounded quite eloquent.

"I went to school with Raine. College. We lived a few doors down from each other. I guess Raine became what I should have to become, successful. But instead…I became a heroin addict. I live in a hospital in upstate New Jersey."

George's mother lowered her head, proud of her son, yet ashamed of his admission. George continued.

"I was so bad off. I nearly died a few times. Put my mother through hell. I'm sorry, mom. I lost the will to live. Even after all the shock treatment and other stuff…there was nothing much to live for. I became a bump on a log. I guess that's what you would call me now…just a bump on a log. And I guess all this happened to me because I didn't much like myself. I didn't really think I was good at anything."

He took a long pause, looked back at the casket, and then turned his attention back at the guests.

"I lost all my friends. They stopped coming around years ago. I mean," he chuckled, "Who wants to visit some bump on a log in a mental hospital, right?"

No one in the church laughed. It was all too painful. George noticed, but chuckled by himself anyway.

"Then one day...a few weeks ago...out of nowhere...comes Raine Addison, the kid that lived a few doors down from me in college. I never saw him after we graduated and moved out of the dorms. I forgot he even existed. Shame on me, I guess. Anyway, Raine shows up out of the blue to come see me. I was too ashamed to talk to him. I was hoping he'd think he had the wrong guy and just leave, but he didn't. I mean, he did...but then he came back a little bit later and caused a huge ruckus in the ward. He ran around naked with a...well, I don't need to go into that. I'm in a church."

He took another long pause. "Anyway, you want to know why he did that? It was because he wanted to hear me laugh."

George looked at the casket again for a moment, and then returned his attention back at the guests. "I found out later...much later...too much later...after Raine died, that he came back because I was the best thing he had ever heard. He wrote me a letter and told me that. My laugh, my ridiculous laugh, was the best thing he'd ever heard in his entire life, and he wanted to hear it just one more time before he...died."

George took a long pause again, contemplating

everything silently as everyone watched.

"I'd never been the best at anything. I always considered myself a failure...until Raine came back. I had no idea I was the best thing he'd ever heard. I never thought I could be someone's best anything, and I guess most of the time no one knows that they are... even if it is just because of a stupid laugh. But we are."

George looked down at the faces in the church. "You might be someone's best," he said pointing to one of Raine's office colleagues. "And you might be someone's best, too," he said pointing to a woman in a pew. "And I guess because of that, whether we know it or not, we are all the best something...for someone. And I am honored to have been the best something for Raine."

George looked at the casket and addressed it. "They're letting me take weekend visits home now, Raine, because I've learned to laugh again. My mom gets to not be so alone anymore in that house."

George's mother took a Kleenex out of her purse and began to weep in it. Claude, who was sitting next to her, put his arm around her.

"You're my best, Raine. And I think it's safe to say you're my mom's best, too. The best thing to ever happen to us."

George lowered his head, shed a few tears, and then walked slowly away from the podium, down the steps and back into the pew where he threw his arms around his mother and wept.

It was now April's turn. She slowly stood, as did Guy. He helped lead her up to the altar and podium, and then stepped away. April looked out at all the faces and managed a smile.

"I had notes with me to help me get through what I wanted to say here today on behalf of my brother, but instead I've decided to read a letter, one of several, apparently, that Raine had written. I think this will truly show the side of Raine he rarely allowed others to see," said April. She then cleared her throat as she opened the letter Mrs. Shapiro had given her and read it aloud.

"I am dying. By the time you read this, I will be dead. A strange way to start a letter, I know, but that's not why I'm writing to you. To put it simply, you were one of the things I've considered "my best." You, Mrs. Shapiro, was the best thing I've ever felt. When you touched the face of that small boy, scared and shaken on the playground all those years ago, I had never felt so comforted and cared for in my life. Your fingers on my cheek, I can only compare to an angel's. A simple gesture that had stayed with me throughout my life, and one I would recall during times when I struggled and felt terribly alone, which, I'm embarrassed to admit, was quite often. I wanted to feel your touch one last time before I died. It is my hope that somehow, without it being too awkward, that I have achieved this. If you are reading this now, then know that I had, and that I am eternally grateful.

April took a deep sigh, and continued reading. "And now I have a favor to ask. I have left my sister, April, all of my possessions, my entire estate, but the only thing she truly wants is to remember me after I am gone. I was an asshole in life. I made a lot of money, and knew everything about business and finance, but not a damn thing about the real meaning of living. But April taught me the meaning in one night, the night of her engagement party. She'll remember. April knows about the important things in life, which makes her way smarter than I ever was."

April's voice cracked. She quickly composed herself, and continued. "So, to help April remember me, I ask that you please attend my funeral. It will no doubt be at Saint John's in Darien, Connecticut. It will be announced in the papers, or you can phone and ask. Please attend, but not on my account, but for April. Introduce yourself and share with her our recent experience together in as much detail as possible. I ask that you do this for those times when she will feel the need to remember me. Please take her call, and have a good laugh at my expense. This way, I'll know April will be taken care of. And maybe, just maybe, I'd had done something worthwhile, and know that my life wasn't as wasted as I'd come to find out. Many thanks, Raine."

April looked down at the letter and bit her lower lip, just like her brother used to, not wanting to give way to her emotions. She thought about how Raine wouldn't like that. He always hated it when she cried, so she wanted to show some kind of restraint...for him.

She then looked up and said slowly, "I've often heard, or read, of people being compared to a stone thrown into pond, and the ripples in the water that come from the stone are how we touch others. I think Raine has proven that comparison because each one of you who has come into contact with one of his ripples has benefitted from it, directly or indirectly, known or unknown. And though he never showed it in life, he showed it today that, yes, he was a good man, and had a good heart."

April lowered her head, and finally allowed her

tears to fall. She then looked at his casket and said in a choked voice, "I love you, Raine, my brother. I love you." She then stepped away from the podium with the help of Guy.

Shortly after, the priest stood before the congregation and lifted his arms, which was a cue for a staff member in the back of the church to begin playing the music.

It was a song chosen by Raine. Jackson Browne's, "Sky Blue and Black," the song that connected him to everything the night he drove Paul home to Brooklyn.

CHAPTER THIRTY-THREE

ALL THE GUESTS WERE AT April's home after the funeral. There was a lot of laughter, a lot of tears, and a lot of love...just as Raine would have wanted it. And everyone enjoyed the delicious pastries Jennifer had made for the occasion, so much so that April insisted she make her wedding cake. That was when Jennifer shared with April Raine's prearrangement for it.

The two women hugged and held each other tight. It was the start of a deep friendship that would last the rest of their lives.

April wanted to hear the stories from those who knew Raine during the short journey that he took. They all exchanged phone numbers and promised to stay in touch. And they all did because Raine was someone worth remembering.

The End

ABOUT THE AUTHOR

LeeAnna Neumeyer is a screenwriter and novelist. She is the author of *Lonely Heart Of The Little Prince*, *Cinderella in Therapy* and the non-fiction eBook, *From Screenplay to Novel*. Ms. Neumeyer is a graduate of the State University of New York at New Paltz with a degree in English. She is currently working on her next novel.